N(
EVERYTHING
CHANGES

ONE MAN'S SEARCH FOR TRUTH
IN A WORLD GONE MAD.

BY STEVE MALTZ

Saffron Planet
PO Box 2215
Ilford IG1 9TR
UK
T: +44 (0) 7885 941848
E: contact@saffronplanet.net

ISBN 978-1-9163437-7-1

NOW
EVERYTHING
CHANGES

Contents

NOW EVERYTHING CHANGES

PART ONE
Derek's Story

1 It's 3am and my brain is ticking over like a stuttering jalopy. I couldn't sleep, which is why I left behind the comforting warmth of my king-size hotel bed beside my gently purring wife, for the small armchair at the corner of the room by the window. I sit there, conflicted and confused, but curiously not tired. I just can't get it out of my mind, the image that summed up my day yesterday, sitting there framed at the centre of my mind in full technicolour glory … But … wait … I am being rude. Let me first introduce myself.

My name is Derek Courtney. Rather a grey, uninteresting individual, well into middle age, peaks of past achievements giving way to troughs of compromise, indecision and fears of impending decrepitude. I am an architect by trade, at the tail end of my career, so content doing the odd consultancy job. I am happily married to Dawn, with a full set of kids and grandkids to provide welcome distraction from … what? That's the question. In fact, should I be asking questions anyway, shouldn't a man of my years have all the answers by now?

Shouldn't I be content with life? After all, grandkids need current investment if I'm to enjoy future dividends? Surely, questions would just get in the way, the last thing this ageing man needs is a fresh challenge. That's a luxury for youth, when life's pathways present themselves, imploring you to travel along their exciting but uncertain corridors. I yearn for sleep, but tiredness is a forlorn hope. My mind is not ready for release and is begging me to deal with the situation. What am I to do? I have not been one to ask too many questions before. Until now, that is. It seems that some spark has flickered into life and I'm not sure that I am adequately equipped to process it. It's time to put you out of your misery, dear reader.

Dawn and I are avid walkers, despite our ageing knees and compromised health fed by ... let's face it ... too much feeding! Nevertheless, we have enjoyed our little nature jaunts since our early days together and see no reason at present to sway from our tradition. We are on a weekend break in the Lake District. Yesterday we visited Ulverston, a favourite of ours as it's always full of life and there's always something going on. It wasn't a particularly favourable visit for us as it seemed a little too full of life, dominated by so many folks of a 'younger persuasion' that we felt really out of it and detached from it all. So, we decided to take a walk to visit a much-loved beauty spot, Hoad Hill, just outside the town and a suitable test for our middle-aged stamina. We arrived there early afternoon and were greeted with a flag proudly swaying in the wind at the summit of the hill. A flag? At first, I thought this was a nod to the nearby monument, a memorial to Sir John Barrow, a renowned explorer. Perhaps it was one of the places he visited? Dawn took a photo and googled the flag. It was the flag of Palestine. Palestine? I didn't even know that it was a country. Anyway, Barrow has only really been associated with South Africa and China. So, Palestine? Has this area been conquered by Palestinians? Neil Armstrong stuck a flag on the moon and explorers stick flags on mountains they have climbed as symbols of their triumph. So, what had Palestine done to warrant this hugely symbolic act?

I don't know why but this really needles me. It seems like an invasion. There's not a racist bone in my body but the thought of anything other than a Union Jack on English soil seems so wrong. Perhaps I am a racist, an unconscious one and this flag has ignited something nasty from within? This troubles me. I have run out of thoughts on the subject and suddenly a wave of tiredness creeps in and pulls me into its world ...

2 Over our buffet breakfast I give a run-down of my nocturnal adventures to Dawn. She is more dismissive than I expected.

"Come on, love. Just one of those things. Not something that should trouble ordinary people like you and me."

I am silent, as I had my tongue wrapped around a mouthful of Cumberland sausage.

"Perhaps you should spend more time thinking of your diet than ... flagpoles."

And that, in a short sentence, defines my wife, my treasured companion through thirty fairly unremarkable years. I love her more now than when we married in that Islington registry office and perhaps the secret to our marital longevity has been the safe path we have both trodden, separately and together. In the great British stoical tradition, we have just 'kept our heads down and got on with it.' Not for us have been midlife crises, seven-year itches, or hormone driven calamities, just a stiff upper lip and cold showers. To her, particularly, the home is a 'divine sanctuary', not to be violated or even taken for granted. It is like a piece of machinery, kept well-oiled by love and good manners. Meal times were as regular as clockwork, visits from family and friends tightly regulated. No cold callers, hawkers, canvassers, religious maniacs. You get the drift. This is her domain and she is the queen of all she surveys. And I was ... and still am ... happy to comply.

"But, Dawn. It has affected me, I have to confess. I don't know why. I just can't put my finger on it."

"Just drink your coffee and go on that app thingy ... there's lots of construction work on the M6, you need to find a new route home ... we really must be home in time for me to cook dinner."

And this for her, is a dismissal and a, frankly clumsy transition to the more important things in life, to her. But I was insistent.

"That flag would have been seen as far as boats on Morecambe Bay. If they wanted to be seen by the most people, that flag was put in exactly the right place ... I wonder why?"

She ignores me. Instead, she gets to her feet and fusses about in her handbag.

"Not for us to worry about ... as I said. Come on Derek ... chop, chop!"

She wanders off but I stay sitting, lost in my thoughts. Then I too get to my feet and mutter to myself.

"Perhaps she's right. She usually is."

I hurry over to the front door to join her, scrolling feverishly on my Google Maps app on the way.

3   The next day there is still this unscratched niggle in the back of my brain. It isn't going to go away in a hurry, so I decide to bring in a new perspective to my predicament. I am sitting in the garden of the Cat's Whisker public house waiting for my best mate, Alf, to reward me with the benefit of his wisdom, now that he's had time to ruminate over the situation.

"Well mate," he says, "there's a news story of a similar thing happening on the east side of London, the borough of Redbridge."

He passes his phone over to me as he supplies commentary.

"It seems that it's partly a gesture of solidarity for the Palestinians in Gaza and partly a political gesture of opposition to the sitting Labour MP, whom they suspect of being on the 'other side' of the conflict."

"Politics leaves me dead, Alf. Voted for the Tories all my life. No idea why, really. Just don't fancy the others."

Alf pats me on my shoulder, as if placating a young child.

"There, there, Derek. Then …" He smiles and looks at me intently. "It's time to grow up."

I take a large swig from my small glass of Guinness and roll it around my mouth before speaking.

"Then educate me."

"Gladly."

"Where do we start?"

"With a drink … your round, Derek."

Alf holds up his empty glass. I quickly swig the dregs and give Alf a ten-pound note. He takes both glasses, leaving his seat. When Alf returns, he finds me sitting upright like a teacher's pet in the classroom, ready and willing to be 'educated'. He places both glasses down and clears his throat, then speaks, in the tones of a crusty old teacher.

"Are you comfortable? …" I nod eagerly. "… then I will begin."

"There seems to be a worldwide movement of solidarity behind the Palestinians in Gaza and other places, in response to what is seen as extreme violence from the Israeli army."

He stops, with a self-satisfied grin.

"And?"

"That's it, mate."

"That's it?"

"That's the limit of my knowledge on the subject, I'm afraid. But at least I got a drink out of you – usually have to beg on my bended knees ..."

Alf gives a triumphant smirk. I'm disappointed.

"Some good you are! I've gathered that much from the news snippets I have seen over the last few months, or perhaps even further back ... in fact ... it seems that this situation's always been there ... is that right?"

"Well, I'm not really the person to ask, Derek. My grasp of this conflict is probably only one step ahead of yours! Like you I've given up even trying to understand it. Is it really important to do so?"

"When flags are raised in beauty spots in our quiet countryside, then perhaps it is."

"Then are you prepared to do so?"

"What?"

"To find out more? To invest a bit of time and effort."

I become a bit pensive and down my drink in one go, lick my lips and speak.

"Yes ... perhaps ... I think I am. Otherwise, I don't think I'm going to get much sleep. I'm that sort of person, I need to see the 'big picture'. It's what I am as an architect, I need to have the whole property in mind, not just a small part of it. The full picture, no loose ends."

"So, mate, how are you going to do this?"

"That I have no clue about."

"Then perhaps I can help you."

Alf winks at me knowingly.

"How about you pop around to mine tomorrow night? There's someone I want you to meet."

He then thinks for a bit.

"Assuming he wants to speak to you."

4 So here I am, the following day, standing outside the door of Alf's semi, no doubt being scanned by his Ring.com doorbell, as I hear its familiar tones chiming away. The door opens. Alf is standing there and gestures for me to enter. The hallway leads to an open-plan lounge-diner. The dining table has the detritus of a small meal. Some wine bottles stand proudly in the centre. To the right of the table is a comfy armchair. Sitting there is a man, middle-aged, with a receding hairline and dark piercing eyes. He is vaguely Middle Eastern in appearance but dressed in the Western manner. He has a glass to his lips, which he immediately sets down on a side table, then stands up to greet me heartedly. Alf introduces us.

"Derek, this is Yusuf ... Yusuf ... Derek."

I offer my hand. Yusuf takes it in both of his and shakes it with great gusto. I am a little taken aback as I prefer to keep strangers at a distance and to bed them in slowly.

Nevertheless, I smile at him and our eyes lock in a friendly manner. Alf passes me a small glass of a dark liquid that I assume is my beloved Guinness and gestures for me to sit on an armchair directly opposite to Yusuf. Then he sits down too on a hard chair to the side of both of us, a glass of white wine in his hand.

"We've just been having an important discussion, Derek," he says.

I am a little taken aback, illogically thinking, *why have they started without me?*

"Oh yes?", I reply, hiding my disappointment.

"Arsenal or Man U for the league this year?"

I gather myself and hold back a bit, reordering my thoughts to counter this unexpected opening.

"Well … um … as you know I'm a Spurs fan, myself. And the last thing I would want is to see Arsenal at the top … so …"

"It's Man U then," shouts Yusuf, a little too loudly in my estimation.

"It's a little too early …"

"Ignore him, Derek. He knows there's no chance. Just give him a bit of glory."

I nod and shrug. I feel a bit awkward so I take a long swig at my drink while they continue to banter for a bit longer. Small talk is definitely not my thing, so I let them continue for a minute or two while I pretend to be interested. Eventually they finish. Evidently an unseen social rule has kicked in and they are now ready to commence … whatever. They both look at me. Alf speaks first.

"Derek here has a question for you, Yusuf."

"Oh yes? Should I be worried, Alf?" he replies, smiling and showing an impressive set of pearly white teeth (I found out later that he was a local dentist of great renown and his winning smile was a key part of his arsenal for putting the nervous at ease).

"No … no …" I stutter. "Of course not."

Alf nods at me to go on.

"Well, OK. Let's see."

My opening salvo is not very impressive. I press on.

"Did Alf tell you about the flag, Yusuf?"

"The flag ... oh yes, he did ..." His smile becomes even broader. "How wonderful!" he adds.

I'm not sure how to respond. Alf helps me out.

"Derek ... I think ... was just shocked to see the flag – of another nation – in this beauty spot."

We both look at Yusuf. His expression hasn't changed, perhaps just a slight air of confusion about him as he tries to inject some humour. He speaks.

"And why not? A thing of beauty ... in a place of beauty."

He can see that I'm not responding in the way that he expects. He continues, a little more seriously.

"And what is wrong with this, Derek? Palestinian flags are appearing all over the country. Your ... our ... country is totally behind us on this. This is what really excites me."

I decide to delve deeper. Perhaps now I will get my question answered. I speak.

"What do you mean 'the country is behind us'? What are we ... behind?"

I spoke that final word with an intentional inflection, to emphasise it.

"My people's struggle against the imperialist colonisers."

There is a lot about this answer that confuses me. Firstly, this evidently integrated Muslim – who even supports Manchester United – is talking about *his* people. And then he is using terms that I haven't heard in conversation since my student days at Essex University, where we all ranted and raved against imperialism and colonisers and such things. I start to unpack my concerns.

"So ... these people ... the Palestinians are ... your people? How does that work out if you don't mind me asking?"

I can see his neck slightly reddening and the tone of his voice is raised very slightly in pitch as he answers.

"I am ... as your friend here knows ... a proud Muslim and ... whenever ... wherever ... I see injustices against my fellow Muslim then I need to ... speak up."

"Oh, I see. And that's how you feel right now?"

"Yes". His voice was definitely becoming a bit more strident. Casual chat about football now seemed like another country. He continues.

"And how can I stay silent when the 'Zionist Entity' is committing genocide against my brothers and sisters."

"Zionist Entity?"

"Israel." Alf had piped up. He then attempts to calm things down a bit.

"Yusuf's people – the Palestinians – have been under the cosh for quite some time now. It's understandable that he should be concerned."

Alf places his hand on Yusuf's shoulder, to reassure him.

"We're all friends here, Yusuf." I take the cue.

"Yes, Yusuf. Consider me a blank slate here. I know nothing about the conflict between the Palestinians and ... Israel. I've come just to get your take on the situation. Can you tell me more ... like the history behind it?"

Yusuf looks at me with a curious expression, as if he considers such a question an affront. I find this strange. Even stranger is his reply.

"We don't go into ... such things." He pauses, as if in thought. Then, recovering a little, he points to me and speaks.

"I'll tell you what, Derek. I'm going into town for a solidarity demonstration on Saturday. We're marching from Trafalgar Square. Come with me, there'll be people there who can answer your questions."

Alf suddenly gets animated.

"What a good idea. Go for it, mate, I think it will finally sort you out and give you a bit of ... y'know ... peace."

I nod faintly, not answering them straight away. I am a bit troubled at how quickly Yusuf had slipped into such an emotional state. Surely I'm not a threat to him but, perhaps, my question was? I eventually agree to meet him there outside the National Gallery at midday. What have I wandered into here? Perhaps I should have kept my head down and not followed my instincts on this. What would Dawn think? I decided that I wasn't going to tell her about my arrangements this Saturday as I know she would have been firmly against it, particularly as we usually spend Saturday afternoons doing a bit of maintenance work in our garden, with Classic FM lulling our mood and the treat of an afternoon tea with scones and strawberry jam. What on earth have I swapped it for? I am worried, but also a new emotion is fighting its way to the surface and it isn't entirely unwelcome. Is it anticipation, a sense of adventure? I'm not sure ... but a part of me suddenly starts to look forward to the next stage of this investigation (of course the rest of me is cowering in a corner, yearning for the comfort of my mother's womb!)

The rest of the evening is unremarkable and pleasantly convivial. We move to other topics; cricket (apparently Yusuf supports the Pakistani team), also food and drink and finish off with some coarse jokes, an Alf speciality, which leaves me outwardly cringing and suppressing my mirth. After all, I am a bit old school and prone to embarrassment, comically betrayed by blushing cheeks unfortunately. This provides as much hilarity as the lurid punchlines. It is something that I was well used to in life and it didn't bother me unduly. I again start thinking about Saturday. Again, mixed feelings fight for supremacy. This is new to me and just a bit disconcerting, but I shrug this off and decide to just go with the flow. *Come on Saturday, bring it on (but be gentle with me)!*

.

5   I arrive at Trafalgar Square a little early. That has always been my style, to always do a recce first, particularly if I am faced with the unfamiliar. And, boy, this is really unfamiliar. It started in the Northern Line train taking me to Trafalgar Square. It was quite packed for a Saturday. From the particular demographic that I observed, it seemed like there was some sort of community celebration event taking place in the West End somewhere. There were many young people, of all hues and appearances, with family groups prevalent, including babies in pushchairs. I ventured a brief smile at a young couple, who smiled back. What a wonderful atmosphere! Perhaps I should abort my mission and join them instead!

I then noticed that many of them had banners with them that were unrolled as we all left the train together at the same destination. I was expecting a Muslim rally, but what I was seeing here was the very picture of multiculturalism. This was a complete surprise. It threw me a bit but it also cheered me as it meant that I wouldn't stand out as much as I had feared. And I am not a person comfortable at standing out. Ask Dawn. I am such a wallflower at parties, that people have mistaken me for ornamental statues. This is just one of her jokes really that she readily repeats at such parties. By contrast, she is a social butterfly on such occasions, which is totally at odds with her normal persona of this dowdy housewife who wouldn't say boo to a goose. We live in a strange world.

It gets stranger when I emerge, blinking, into the mid-day sun. It is like early morning at a street market. People are setting up stalls around the periphery. But these stalls aren't for fruit & veg, or clothing or bric-a-brac, instead they are piled high with banners and posters, and manned by dubious individuals who could be cloned from the reactionaries I had known from the '60s. There is not a Muslim in sight as far as I can see, instead I see logos and decals for the Socialist Workers Party, the Communist Party, Socialists for Palestine and others. Again, a flashback to 1968, the year of revolutionary fervour and student agitation.

These people, surely, are at the wrong demo. Perhaps I had accidentally stumbled upon some kind of hub, from where protest groups fan out. I look closer at the banners and realise that, indeed, I am at the right place. *Zionism is Fascism, Israel Apartheid, Free Palestine, Boycott Israel, From the River to the sea…, We will wipe out Israel.*

I am horrified. This is not so much a demonstration of support for the oppressed, but more a gesture of unbridled hatred for the perceived oppressors. Why would this be? And what is the connection between the Far Left of the communists and socialists and the religious system represented by the Muslim Palestinians? I had come here to be educated and enlightened, but all that confronts me is unbridled emotionalism and, for a sober, awkward Englishman like myself, this is indeed an alien land. And then the chanting starts …

I am offered leaflets. I take one and see that it is actually a card of instructions on what to do if arrested! A peaceful demo? What have I stumbled on here? Already, Dawn's cream tea never felt more enticing, as I did an about-turn to return to the sanctuary of the London Underground. And I would have made it if Yusuf hadn't spotted me first.

"Derek," he cries, "not leaving already? It hasn't even started yet ... Come!"

He leads me through the crowds that are being sporadically spewed out of the tube station, but also pouring into the square from all directions. The chanting was increasing in volume and I can see a young Muslim girl with a megaphone leading the proceedings. The crowd, by now, is predominantly Muslim as I could see from the dress and behaviour, but there are a fair smattering of white faces, mostly young – Generation Z I believe – but with a few greybeards and straggly hairs, relics from days that perhaps we all thought were thankfully long forgotten.

"Come and meet Rahima," Yusuf says, as he pulls me to the edge of the crowd and onto the steps of St Martins in the Fields Church on the west side of the Square. She is young, very young, perhaps in her early 20s and dressed in a full burka, only her eyes showing. She must have been quite beautiful if her eyes were a signpost for the rest of her. They are blue-green and so alive and passionate. In fact, they just about describe her as a person, as I am soon to find out.

"Rahima, this is the man I spoke about, my neighbour's friend, Derek."

"Salaam Alaikum, Derek."

I nod and smile. I don't attempt the Arabic greeting, scared of getting it wrong.

"Isn't this a fine turnout, Derek?" she adds.

"Impressive number … must be in the thousands."

"Tens of thousands "adds Yusuf, as if he has been counting.

"Right, brother" she agrees, "And so many of them … your brothers and sisters."

She nods at me when she says this.

"Yes," I added, "Plenty of non-Muslims it seems, Rahima. I saw a lot of them giving out placards. They remind me of my student days back in the '70s …"

She appears not to be listening. She's distracted, perhaps by the atmosphere, which was, to me, getting more menacing by the minute. She senses my discomfort.

"You're safe here, Derek."

She pauses and examines me a little closer. "You're not Jewish are you, Derek?"

I shake my head.

"Does it matter?"

"Oh yes … it matters. But I can tell you're not Jewish … you seem normal … safe … simple even."

I start to feel even more uncomfortable. It is time to ask questions. After all, this is why I had come here. I have to take back some positives from a situation that is sinking by the second.

"Rahima, can I ask you a question?"

"Go ahead, Derek. This is why we are talking, is it not?"

Her bright eyes seem to flash a little and they narrow slightly as if poised for … attack?

"Why are these demonstrations necessary? I have to be frank but the atmosphere here ... it's so heavy ... what are you trying to achieve with the marching and the chanting and the ..."

"Let me stop you there and ask you a question, Derek. I am not expecting an honest answer as ... I suspect ... that you may be part of the problem ... rather than the solution."

"How? Why?" I stutter, taken aback by the new direction of this conversation.

"You're British, right ... and white ... right?" She smirks at Yusuf, at least that's what her eyes conveyed. He smirks back and speaks.

"You can't possibly understand the plight of our Palestinian brothers and sisters. You're a colonialist, your great-grandparents were probably part of the slave trade ..."

"The Patriarchy!" she adds. "I bet the women in your family were oppressed ... and your family was probably less than pleased when the 'coloureds' started invading your cosy white paradise."

"Excuse me?" I am a little riled ... and it takes a lot to ignite a flame of indignancy from within my passive persona.

"Why are you here, Derek?" she mocks. "To report back to your 'mates in the pub' about these deluded maniacs you have met ...?"

"No. How can you say that, Rahima? I am honestly seeking the truth. I came here to find out more about the conflict and why you hate Israel ... and the Jews too, looking at some of the banners here. Where does it come from?"

Rahima looks at Yusuf and they both seem to have come to a decision. The atmosphere suddenly changes, perhaps turned down a notch or two. She smiles. I could see it in her eyes.

"My sincere apologies, Derek. I think we have got you wrong. Sorry for jumping down your throat. Yes, it is all a bit charged up here." She bows her head very slightly and I appreciate this.

I sit down on the steps of the church. She sits next to me. We are facing the growing crowds, a number that stretches as far as the eye can see.

"Look at this, Derek" she says, gesturing to the crowds. "There must be a good reason for such a turnout. They can't all be wrong ... or 'deluded.'"

I nod in agreement.

"Let me give you a history lesson. Then you'll understand us a bit better, I think."

I sigh with relief. This is what I had come for. My investigation that began with that Palestinian flag is possibly going to reach some sort of resolution. This is my hope as I don't think that I could deal with any more intensity and passion. It is just not in my nature. Dawn had a pet name for me, only used on certain occasions when she wished to make a point. The 'spent volcano', someone who has long ago rid himself of the passions and intrigues of youth and has settled down into safe predictability. To be honest, it has been so long since this particular volcano was active, that any memory of it has long since faded. Do I see some embers about to flicker back into life? I hope not. She begins.

"We called it the Nakba, in 1948, when we were violently expelled from our homeland by Jewish terrorist gangs, held together by a colonialist idea called Zionism. We still hold on to the noble and righteous dream to return to our land, where we have lived for many centuries ..."

I felt I had to interrupt.

"Excuse me, Rahima. You say 'we' ... are you a Palestinian?"

"No ... I'm from Bradford. I say 'we' because ..."

She looks around.

"We are all Palestinians here!"

I nod thoughtfully as she continues.

"The Israelis are still there, in our land and still seeking to expand it – like in Gaza. We Palestinians represent all colonial victims everywhere, our struggle is ... their struggle. In particular we represent the true Arab and Muslim identity. We contrast this with the 'Jewish' state, calling itself a democracy but practising apartheid with brutish violence. We must continue to resist this and bring other like minds into the resistance, until we can bring about a true revolution. Palestinians, a peace-loving people of such talent, culture and history, have to be allowed to regain their position in society. Of course, the world does not believe us – preferring to believe the Israeli 'narrative' and Jewish lies. This is why ... this ... is needed, Derek."

This seems like a prepared speech, littered with slogans but I just put this down to excitable youth and don't comment. To do so would definitely have lit a fuse! I can now see a connection with those people I saw earlier, the promoters from the far left, the people who reminded me of the student agitators from my youth. You don't have to be a genius to pick out the trigger words.

I remain quiet, as if mulling over the words. In truth, I am disturbed by what I heard from her and what I am seeing around me. Perhaps it is my lack of response, or perhaps she is bored with me as her attention seems to be elsewhere now as she points something out to Yusuf and they both just drift into the crowd, leaving me alone with my thoughts.

I am horrified as I seem to be wading through a sea of extremist politics here. I expected to witness a peaceful rally, with legitimate demands put forwards for discussion and an atmosphere of communal well-being and worthiness. Instead, I am a part of a hate-filled cauldron, a place that a quiet, unassuming person like me would only read about in the papers, not actually be a part of. I can see TV cameras dotted around and hope against hope that out of the thousands of faces here, mine won't be one of those selected for broadcast. What if Dawn is watching the TV news and sees me here? How would I explain myself? It would be like being caught red-handed in some sordid affair or trolling the streets for 'ladies of the night' or worse!

I decide to move. Not now towards the tube station but rather further into the mass of excited human beings. A part of me wants to find out more, my appetite has been whetted. I am not satisfied with what I had heard so far and with what I could see. I want to know why tens of thousands of what seems to be mostly ordinary people would give up their gardens or TVs or picnics in the park to come here to vent their anger. I look around. Next to me is a small Muslim family group, including two young children. The father is pointing his phone camera at a young boy, who is holding up a banner, 'From the River to the Sea, Palestine shall be free' and chanting the words. It is clear that he has no idea what he is doing but his family is encouraging him as if he was taking part in an innocent game rather than espousing a slogan that, as I found out later, was promoting genocide.

Does everyone feel that way here? I keep moving. Something

to my left catches my eye, something that looks unbelievably out of place in this particular gathering. It is a group of identifiably Jewish men, dressed as orthodox versions of their faith. I can't believe this. Are they mad? Are they here to incite the crowd to violence? I have to investigate, so I inch over to where they gather in a small group at the south west side of the Square. A further shock is in store for me when their banner came into view, *Free Palestine.* Another declared, *Judaism condemns the State of Israel and its atrocities.*

I am astounded. Here are a group of very overt Jews, complete with bushy beards and massive circular hats. I am too dumbfounded and tongue-tied to speak to them. Instead, I take a leaflet from an elderly Jew whose defining feature is spittle in his straggly beard, perhaps from too much shouting. They are a fringe Jewish sect called *Neturei Karta,* who oppose the modern State of Israel, though their grounds are firmly religious through their interpretation of their own holy books. This is intriguing. Within the space of a few minutes I have encountered two sets of people, as widely apart from each other as it is possible to be in the cultural spectrum, yet united by hate ... of Israel. Jews hating other Jews? Don't they have enough enemies, without making enemies of each other? You couldn't make it up!

The thought that I had kept suppressed since this whole thing started with me in the Lake District, finally came to the surface. *What has Israel done to attract such hatred?* Is there a basis for it? Can tens of thousands of people be so wrong, even though at least a significant number are what I would term anarchists, who would find good reason to hate just about everyone! I know that I probably won't get answers today, but I know that I am in the right place to be at least asking some questions. In fact, I feel quite emboldened to do so, I have no idea why. This whole issue now has a grip on me. It is a familiar feeling, a common feature of my days as an architect working for a thriving and aggressive partnership, where problems were just solutions in the making. I now know that I have to see this through to the end.

6 Speeches had been made and the march had begun towards the Mall, ending up with a massive rally in Hyde Park, with more speeches by Labour MPs and Islamic scholars. Again, the incompatibility of backgrounds hits me. (I learn later that this was called cognitive dissonance, a feature of the confusing culture that now held sway, where you are free to believe just about anything even if it contradicts everything else you believe in. What a world!)

Where was Margaret Thatcher when you needed her? I am confronted by, I suppose, a comical example of this, though I must confess feeling very sorry for the fellow in question.

Here is a small blonde youth, perhaps a teenager, evidently gay and carrying a banner, 'Queers for Palestine'. He seems to be alone and I suppose I feel both sorry for him and unthreatened by him, so I speak to him.

"Hello. You look a bit lonely. Can I ask you a question?"

He hesitates for a moment, sizing me up. I suppose I am a little straight-laced for him, making him a tad suspicious. But he shrugs and speaks.

"OK. Mate. Fire away."

"Why are you here? You seem a bit out of place."

His hackles are raised.

"What d'you mean? Are you being homophobic, mate?"

"No, no ... that's my point ... from my limited knowledge I remember reading a news story ... or was it a YouTube video ... about gay people being thrown from buildings in Gaza."

"That's what the Zionists do! They hate everyone, especially people like me."

"No ... not the Israelis, the Palestinians ... gays are not welcome, it's a religious thing I think."

He ignores me, but I could see a tinge of panic in his eyes. Does his banner visibly droop a few inches then?

"And Israel ... I think ... again, I'm sure I've read it somewhere ... is one of the most gay-friendly places in the world."

He stops and stares at me, thinks for a bit, then speaks, loudly.

"So what! Palestine must be free! Queers for Palestine!"

He moves on, ignoring me. He evidently hadn't thought this thing through, but perhaps I had given him food for thought for the future? Who knows! I think that I have followed Alice into Wonderland, where everything is skewed and upside down and inside out. I carry on. I see a young white couple, fairly well dressed, pushing a pushchair. They have no banner, neither are they chanting slogans. The pushchair, though, is resplendent with stickers, addressing issues like veganism, animal welfare, climate change and pollution. I feel that they would be safe to speak to, I might even learn something.

"Hello there."

They smile at me. They have open faces, people of both words and action, I think. The man answers.

"Hi! Isn't this great?"

My heart sinks. I feel like I have been here before.

"Yes", I stammer, not sure what tone to take, so remaining as neutral as I can.

"It's important to support society's victims, don't you think?"

"Yes", I answer, wondering why my brain had somehow disconnected.

"It's at times like this that, with our white privilege, we have to stand and be counted, eh?"

"Um ... yes ... white privilege?"

"Where have you been, fellow, in the past few years. We ... white people ... have had it too good for too long now ... to the detriment of ... others."

His wife nods feverishly in agreement. Again, I feel lost for words, so just nod too.

"Too right!" I answer. *Come on, say something sensible*, I castigate myself.

"Are you into the Palestinian cause, then?" I ask.

"We're into ALL causes", she pipes up, "Isn't that so, darling?"

"Too right," adds her husband. "Our Palestinian brothers and sisters need all the help and support we can give them. We owe them that much."

"But what about the Jews? Does helping the Palestinians mean we should ... hate the Jews?"

"Well, they brought it all on themselves!"

This comes from his wife and every word is spat out as if they were bullets. Her husband nods and gives me a faint smile. They move on, apparently our discussion was now at an end. As I was to find out later, Lenin had a phrase for people like this, *useful idiots*, those who could be duped into following causes that they had absolutely no idea about. I think I had had enough. I had come here for answers, but it seems that, in such an emotionally charged atmosphere, reasoned debate was certainly not on the menu. What have I learned from this little jaunt? Not much, except to fill me full of despair about a world where emotions trump everything. There were so many more questions to ask, but this is evidently not the place to do so.

7 Dawn is sitting opposite me at the breakfast table, eyeing me very suspiciously. Does she believe my excuse for my absence yesterday, or did she see right through me, as is her wont, having endured me for decades and probably wise to all of my "tells"? An afternoon in the library is not the most imaginative of excuses, let's face it!

"Don't forget. Dentist at 10am."

It wasn't something to forget, my visits to Dr Ahmed have been extremely frequent, ever since I had my temporary implants plumbed in a few weeks back and now I have managed yet again to fracture the bridge, needing a quick repair job. This was the second time this week. I wait to see if Dawn has anything to add and then I get up to make a quick exit. It is then that she speaks.

"How's the research going?"

"Fine," I answer, perhaps a little too quickly, despite being the bearer of a little white lie.

But, of course, 'research' doesn't have to involve dusty old books. She nods and I thought that this was my signal to leave.

"Mavis said that you were nowhere to be found in the library. Have you changed libraries, Derek?"

I have a decision to make. Either an outright lie, or the uncomfortable truth. I choose the latter because ... that's just the person I am, really. Quite uncomplicated, though recent intrigues threaten to change this particular status.

"Are you reading me here, Dawn?"

"Depends on if *you* have been doing any reading, love."

There is a sternness there, perhaps with a soupcon of playfulness.

"You're an open book to me."

I take the cue and tell her everything. She is silent throughout and doesn't really say much when I've finished.

"That's nice, Derek ... I suppose it's out of your system now?"

She says this more as a statement than a question and clearly considers the matter closed as it was then that she turned her back and started the washing up.

I leave the room and enter my study, a tiny boxroom at the front of the house, just barely big enough for some shelving and a desk for my computer. I sit on my comfortable swivel chair and ... swivelled ... as my befuddled mind does the same.

"Dr Ahmed," I suddenly exclaimed to no-one in particular. "He's a Muslim!"

What I meant was that my dentist, with whom I have shared many pleasantries since my treatment started all of those weeks ago, was a Muslim, but of the moderate variety, in contrast to my recent experiences. Perhaps I can get his opinion? This seemed sensible at the time, though there is a fear at the back of my mind that one person you wouldn't want to get the wrong side of is one's dentist. Too much capacity to inflict pain! Of course, Yusuf was also a dentist and I wouldn't put it past him to 'accidentally' spike my gums if he felt I was disrespecting his views! Yet he was a professional and I'm sure his feelings wouldn't impinge on his working life. I brush these thoughts aside. My investigation must take priority. regardless.

So here I am, leaning back on the dentist's chair with Dr Ahmed peering thoughtfully at me, his mask insulating me from any emotions he may have, though his eyes are impassive and full of concentration. He is busy applying this white glue to my bridge and sealing it with a heat pen.

"There … all done," he suddenly exclaims, throwing his tools into a ceramic bowl. "Ten minutes early. Well done me!"

I smile after gently running my tongue over the battle site with satisfaction and relief. Then, an idea occurs to me. This, surely, is the opening I needed. As he slips off his mask and levers my chair back, I clear my throat and speak.

"Dr Ahmed. Do you have a few minutes?"

I then proceed to ask my question and wait for a response. In fact I wait so long, I wonder whether there would actually be a response. But, in fact, he was just gathering his thoughts. Then he speaks.

"You call me a 'moderate Muslim,' Mr Courtney and … I've been thinking … is there such a thing? You're either a Muslim … or not a Muslim … Yes, there are extremists out there … and I wonder if they could be seen as Muslims anyway … Now … I know what you are asking … My views on Gaza and Palestine … Well … it's a good question, but a hard question to answer."

"Yes, I'm sorry to put you on the spot and … I know there's not much time to deal with this. Just a few pointers really."

"I understand. So … this is not particularly considered … Just from my gut really … But there are things I can say for certain …

One ... Hamas are NOT Muslim in my view and remembering October 7th ... that was horrific for everyone but more so for us Muslims, as it seemed to be in my name. It was an inexcusable act ... but ... nothing happens in a vacuum ..."

He shrugs and seems to be asking me to read between the lines. It is becoming awkward. He speaks again.

"There are some loud, insistent voices out there ... and they don't speak for us all ..."

He stops and then starts to ready himself for his next patient.

"That's all I can say for now ... we will talk again, maybe."

"OK. Thanks, Dr Ahmed. Sorry to bring this up ... you're a busy man and you're in your workplace ... Inexcusable really."

I leave the surgery, wondering if I had learned anything new..

8 Later that day I had an appointment with a client, to give an estimate for some possible work. It was for an elderly lady (well actually just a few years older than me), a Mrs Martin. Her house was an end-of-terrace in a middle-class area. I arrive promptly, as ever, at 2pm. She greets me with a smile. It is what I would call a sincere smile, rather than one conjured up out of duty. She genuinely seems pleased to see me and already my day is brightened up and my problems shoved onto the back burner. She leads me to her living room and shows me some plans she had made about alterations she needed on the ground floor, involving the re-alignment of the rooms and the addition of an extension. All grist to the mill for me, nothing new here though for her, considering the costs that would be involved, very much a major deal. I am determined to be sensitive to her needs.

It is a straightforward consultation for me and she seems pleased with my input. We also have a pleasant conversation about this and that, as you do, but then … I notice something curious on her mantelpiece. It is one of those Jewish lampstands, that I think they use in one of their festivals, but I couldn't remember what they were called. There was nothing else in the room that indicated that she was Jewish, apart from some framed Psalms hanging on the wall. I point it out to her. She seems pleased about this.

"It's a Chanukiah", she says. "It's used at the Jewish festival of Chanukah, at the end of the year."

"Are you Jewish, Mrs Martin, if you don't mind me asking?"

"No, but my husband is. We are Christians."

"How can a Jew be a Christian? That's interesting."

"Oh it is, but perhaps it shouldn't be. Jesus was Jewish, you know."

"How interesting."

I feel a peculiar tingling sensation and a slight shudder. How strange. Something is going on here. It looks like my investigation is on again!

"You're looking a bit peaky, Mr Courtney. I'll make us both a cup of tea and some biscuits. Are you in a hurry to leave?"

"That would be nice and … no … in fact I have plenty of time."

Over a mug of tea and an unlimited supply of biscuits, Mrs Martin is able to give me some straightforward answers to the questions that are floating around in my brain. She is not, obviously, able to give me much in the way of the Muslim position on Israel, or to comment on some of the strange conversations I have had at Trafalgar Square. But she gives me the assurance that my quest is an honourable one and commends me on my perseverance and open-mindedness. I write a few notes during our visit and here's a summary of them.

The Jews have been around for thousands of years and Judaism predates Islam by many centuries. Jews have been in the contested land far longer than any other people, so to call them colonialists is a bit rich. Yet there were Arab Muslims in the land when the State of Israel was created in 1948 and, since then there have been two incompatible points of view as to what happened next, right up to modern times. That is the heart of the conflict. At Trafalgar Square I only heard one side, but there is a very different alternative view. She didn't consider herself an expert on this but had a friend, a rabbi, who could help. She gave me his details.

So, the journey continues. This stage involves a visit to Rabbi Jacobs, at Bryon Park Reformed Synagogue, in Romford, Essex.

"Let me ask you a question first, Mr Courtney, a hypothetical one."

The rabbi is young, very earnest and evidently pleased to see me. Non-Jews had given the synagogue a wide berth in recent days because of the troubles in the Middle East (apart from those who had daubed swastikas on the outside wall) and so my visit here is both rare and welcome for him.

I gesture for him to continue.

"Let's imagine you live in a small village, separated from a second village by a river. The two villages are natural enemies and there is no contact between the two. They live in a state of peace until … a gang of marauders from village A one day cross the river with murderous intent. They massacre a large number of men, women and children in village B and capture a smaller number, taking them back to village A as hostages. Here's the question ... what is the immediate priority for the leaders in Village B?"

"Tend to the injured, bury the dead and do what they can to get the hostages back."

"Correct. And how do they do that?"

"Ask for them back? Threaten reprisals?"

"That's an option. But the leaders of Village A declare that there is no way they would return the hostages. In fact, they even state that they would do it again and again ..."

"They must really hate Village B."

"Correct. But we won't go there ... yet. So, what other options are there for bringing back the hostages?"

"Fetch them back ... forcibly. I suppose ... but that would mean an invasion ... and war."

"Correct. There's no other option. But there's a snag ... those who kidnapped the hostages are hiding both themselves and the hostages among ordinary villagers, such as in hospitals and places of worship."

"Why is that a snag, Rabbi?"

"Because fetching the hostages back is going to result in civilian casualties."

"But that's what happens in war, I suppose. How else are they going to get them back?"

"And what does this tell you about the kidnappers, hiding among the civilian population?"

"Cowards and ... indifferent to the fate of the ordinary citizens."

"Correct ... in a nutshell. That is Israel and Gaza."

I think for a bit as I connect the stories together.

"But Rabbi. The demonstrators and the newspapers and ... I think ... the United Nations ... they all talk about genocide ... how Israel is targeting civilians with murderous intent."

"Yes they are. They see what they want to see. Now cast your mind back to the demonstration you went to. Did you see and hear the words 'From the River to the Sea, Palestine shall be free'?"

"Oh yes, Rabbi. It must have been the persistent theme."

"Do you know what it refers to and what it implies?"

"Not really."

"The river is the River Jordan; the sea is the Mediterranean. Do you know what country lies in that region?"

"Palestine ... Israel?"

His tone gets a little more strident. His emotions, kept at bay up to this point, are now coming to the surface.

"It's Israel, Mr Courtney ... they want it to be Palestine ... in place of Israel. And do you know what this implies?"

I think for a bit. I think I probably had the answer, but I don't want to take away his thunder.

"No."

He looks at me square in the eyes.

"Genocide ... they would want to see all Jews to go away ... killed ... to be driven into the sea. If you have any doubts about this, go on the Internet and google the Hamas charter, their 'reason for their existence.' Article seven ... a quote from their holy book, 'The Day of Judgement will not come until Muslims fight the Jews, when the Jews will hide behind stones and trees. The stones and trees will say O Muslim, O servant of God, there is a Jew behind me, come and kill him' …"

There is a silence when we both gather our thoughts. The rabbi is visibly upset.

"Don't just consider Hamas … think of the others at that rally … even though they don't realise or understand it … they all want to kill us, Mr Courtney. Genocide is their one and only intention … and yet they accuse Israel of it …"

I don't know what to say. My spirit is in anguish. I'm not Jewish but I know enough about recent Jewish history, the Holocaust, to see a persistent theme here, acted out not just in Nazi Germany and the Middle East but actually on the streets of London.

"Rabbi, I am so sorry. What can I do?"

He looks at me and says these words.

"Follow the evidence … and act on it."

10 The days that followed were a bit of a haze. I had crossed the Rubicon and there was no going back. My emotions had been stirred up and it seems that, after a lifetime of living under the parapet, I now had an issue nagging at my heart. Follow the evidence … and act on it.

What did he mean by these words? Of course, I could skim through the byways of the internet, but it is reality I yearn for, not noise and opinion. I need facts, truth. I've been told that two alternative narratives describe the origins of the situation in the Middle East, but they can't both be right. Something within me tells me that this is just a symptom of something a lot deeper and, however much I claw at it, it is no more than vapour. There is no substance, as of yet. This is what I think he means by following the evidence. So I carry on and follow whatever evidence that presents itself but then what? Act on it? I am not a man of action; remember I am no more than a 'spent volcano'. This brings me back to Dawn. She finds me in the living room, slumped on my favourite armchair, staring at the wall. She sits next to me and gently places her hand on mine.

"Still on your ... investigation?"

I look at her wistfully, hoping that my silence would answer this question.

"It's getting to you, isn't it?"

I nod.

"What we need is a stiff drink and ... together ... let's work things through, love."

There were two surprises in that statement. Firstly, the fact that, regarding our drinks cabinet, even the dust had dust on it. We haven't had a stiff drink since the birth of our daughter, Maisie. And, as for working things out together, I could trace the last time probably to the *conception* of our daughter, Maisie, though that may be a slight exaggeration.

She returns with two whisky macs, our favourite drink from an earlier epoch. I sip mine and immediately memories flood back, a bit jumbled, but all tinged with a carefree bonhomie that now seems a memory from the past. The present has suddenly provided many fresh challenges, to say the least!

She sits next to me, pats down her pinafore and speaks.

"I too have been doing some thinking."

I look at her with amazement. She seems sincere, this isn't a joke, not that she was that type of person anyway. I am most intrigued as to what was on her mind.

Apparently quite a lot.

"Go on," I said.

"Well ... you know I'm a part of a Book club, don't you?"

"Of course, but you've been going for yonks, why bring it up now?"

"Why do you think?"

"Don't know. Tell me."

It is all so stilted and cryptic. I just want her to get to the point but she is clearly playing with me.

"Well ... it just so happens that what we've been reading recently is ... relevant."

She pauses but I let her continue.

"Just after you started your ... investigation ... In the very next meeting they decided to study ... the same subject ... the Middle East and all that."

I am now paying full attention. Are our private worlds going to finally collide?

"In fact, we went through a small booklet together just yesterday. Here, I have a copy for you."

She hands me the booklet, around eight pages, with a bright blue title, *The Simple Guide to the Conflict in the Middle East.* She continues.

"It's a fascinating read and ... I think it may answer a lot of your questions. I'll leave you with it now ... then we can chat."

So, I started reading ...

11 The Simple Guide to the Conflict in the Middle East

How many times have you been approached by someone and asked the question, "So what do you think about what's happening in the Middle East"? How frustrated have you been in your inability to string together a few coherent words, let alone a solid, robust argument to support your views? You are not alone, hours of study and a PhD seem to be the minimum requirements here for a full understanding of the intricacies and subtleties of a situation that doesn't even have a history that people can agree on.

There is nothing more confusing than the Israel/Palestinian conflict. Millions of words have been written and spoken about it, but how much of it has truly sunk in, how much of it has made sense and how much of it has been untainted by personal opinion or editorial slant? Jews and Zionists will tell you one thing and Arabs and Arabists will tell you the opposite! Surely they can't both be right, surely there can only be one truth, one set of proven historical events that can unravel the whole mess. Unfortunately, it isn't that straightforward. The situation is so complex, puzzling and emotionally charged that it is well-nigh impossible to get an objective viewpoint – it is exceedingly difficult to find historical sources with no 'axes to grind', commentators who could be accepted as truly impartial. Nevertheless, please indulge me over the next few minutes, while I try to unravel the mystery, sweep away the web of confusion, set my course for the heart of the matter and try to make sense of it all.

There are two main issues to look at. Firstly, who really owns the land, particularly the area known as the 'West Bank' and, secondly, what is the origin of the Palestinian refugee situation?

Let's first go back to the 19th Century and look at the 'lie of the land'. Palestine, as it was called then (a name given by the Romans in the 1st Century in an effort to remove any Jewish associations with the land) was a poor country, ruled by absentee Turkish landlords, as part of the crumbling and corrupt Ottoman empire. By all accounts the land was largely barren and uninhabited, its population was either nomadic or largely involved with agriculture, despite the poor environment. Sir John William Dawson, writing in 1888, said, "*No national union and no national spirit has prevailed there. The motley impoverished tribes which have occupied it have held it as mere tenants at will, temporary landowners, evidently waiting for those entitled to the permanent possession of the soil*" (Modern Science in Bible Lands - New York 1890 - pp. 449-450). In 1835, Alphonse de Lamartine wrote, "*Outside the gates of Jerusalem we saw indeed no living object, heard no living sound, we found the same void, the same silence ...*" (Recollections of the East, Vol I (London 1845) pp 268).

Thanks to the Turks, the land had been totally neglected. Hundreds of years of abuse had turned the country into a treeless waste, with malaria-ridden swamps, a sprinkling of towns and an unliveable desert in the south. This was the position in 1880, and this is an incontestable fact.

But now we start to get discrepancies. How many people DID live in the land at that time, and WHO were they? Jewish sources put the figure at between 100,000 and 250,000. Arab sources put the figure at about 480,000 (456,000 Arab, 24,000 Jewish). And who were these Arabs? Arab sources would simply say that these were indigenous people, Arabs who have lived in this land for generations. Jewish and independent sources say otherwise. They would point to immigrations from Egypt (to escape heavy taxes), Algeria, Turkey and elsewhere. There are suggestions that up to 25% of the Muslim population were immigrants.

A final word here from the author of 'Tom Sawyer" and "Huckleberry Finn". According to the American author Mark Twain's independent eye-witness account in 1867, "The Innocents Abroad", the land was barely populated, just a collection of small villages in a dry, barren land. This complete book is available on the Internet, so you can check it for yourself. Here's his summary.

"Of all the lands there are for dismal scenery, I think Palestine must be the prince ... It is a hopeless, dreary, heart-broken land ... Palestine sits in sackcloth and ashes. Over it broods the spell of a curse that has withered its fields and fettered its energies ... Nazareth is forlorn; about that ford of Jordan where the hosts of Israel entered the Promised Land with songs of rejoicing, one finds only a squalid camp of fantastic Bedouins of the desert; Jericho the accursed, lies a mouldering ruin, to-day, even as Joshua's miracle left it more than three thousand years ago ... Renowned Jerusalem itself, the stateliest name in history, has lost all its ancient grandeur, and is become a pauper village ... Capernaum is a shapeless ruin; Magdala is the home of beggared Arabs; Bethsaida and Chorazin have vanished from the earth ... Palestine is desolate and unlovely. And why should it be otherwise? Can the curse of the Deity beautify a land?" ..." (The Innocents Abroad (New York 1966) summary of Palestine visit)

Palestine was simply an outpost of the corrupt and decaying Turkish Ottoman Empire. It was not a country or a state in the manner of, say, an England or Germany at that time. It was simply a collection of villages that happened to exist within the geographical region known as Palestine. Although many Arabs

41

did own their own homes, the majority was the poor "fellahin," who worked as hired hands for the landowners. There was no nationalism in the land, no feeling of belonging to a "people", loyalty was to the local clan or village. Arabs did not see themselves as "Palestinians" and often referred to their homeland as Southern Syria.

Jews had always lived in the land right from biblical times, though, in the 19th Century, they were very much the minority. The first major wave of Jewish immigration started in the 1880s and, by the end of the 19th Century, the Jewish population had tripled to over 80,000 (Arab sources).

This included the foundation of the Jewish settlement of Rishon-le-Zion, where 40 Jewish families settled - followed later by more than 400 Arab families from Egypt and elsewhere. This was a community that worked and was at peace. The Arabs saw the benefits of what the Jews were doing to the land and joined them. Between 1882 and 1914 pioneering Jews started, slowly, to transform the land. They worked on the swamps and the undrained rivers. Life was tough, if you didn't die of malaria, you could be killed by Bedouins. Soon Jewish villages were springing up all over, and the towns of Jerusalem, Tiberias, Safed and Haifa started to grow. In 1909 they founded the first modern Jewish city, Tel Aviv. Life was still tough, although disease wasn't so much the problem. Attacks by Arab neighbours increased, even though, through the efforts of these Jewish pioneers, life for all in the land was improving - including the Arab neighbours.

Newspapers and other media sources today give the impression that Israel "occupies" land once owned by people living in a "Palestinian state". But the evidence is to the contrary. For a start, the Arabs in no way saw themselves as "Palestinians".

When the First Congress of Muslim-Christian Associations met in Jerusalem in February 1919, the agreement was that "we consider Palestine as part of Arab Syria". The only people who considered themselves "Palestinians" in the first half of the 20th century were the Jewish inhabitants! Even the Jewish national newspaper was called "The Palestine Post" (now called "The Jerusalem Post").

The other point concerns ownership of the land. Did Jewish immigrants seize it or was the land acquired legally? Land settled in by these first immigrants in the 1880s was bought from the absentee Turkish landlords, who were eager for the extra cash. The land initially settled in was the uncultivated swampy cheap and empty land. Later on they bought cultivated land, some of it at exorbitant prices. In his memoirs, King Abdullah of Jordan wrote "... the Arabs are as prodigal in selling their land as they are in useless wailing and weeping". Up until 1948, with the formation of the State of Israel, no land was seized or acquired in any way other than through legal means.

In the 20th Century, Arabs as well as Jews were immigrating into Palestine, mainly from Egypt, Transjordan, Syria and Lebanon. Between 1922 and 1931 illegal Arab immigrants comprised almost 12% of the Arab population. The Hope Simpson Report acknowledged in 1930 that there was an "*uncontrolled influx of illegal immigrants from Egypt, Transjordan and Syria*". The rate of immigration increased during the early 1930s, which was a period of prosperity in Palestine. The Syrian Governor of Hauran admitted in 1934 that 30,000-36,000 people from his district entered Palestine that year and settled there. In 1939, Winston Churchill said "*Far from being persecuted, the Arabs have crowded into the country and multiplied until their population has increased more than even all world Jewry could lift up (increase) the Jewish population"*. This is an important (though much contested) point, because it dispels the myth that the Palestinian people have lived there for generations. When we talk about Palestinian refugees, displaced as a result of the formation of the State of Israel, consider how many of them would have been as recent to the land as the Jews themselves!

So now we reach that magic date, 1948, the formation of the State of Israel. And the major point of contention – the Palestinian refugees.

This is where objectivity flies out of the window and we get the sharpest divide in people's perceptions of actual historical events. In a nutshell, what happened was that the day after Israel became a country, it was invaded by Egypt, Transjordan, Syria, Lebanon and Iraq.

Within 2 weeks, against all odds, Israel was victorious, resulting in an expansion of territory and the displacement of hundreds of thousands of Arabs who had been living in Palestine.

As a result of these events not one but two refugee situations were created.

Just under 750,000 Arabs (U.N. estimate) lost their homes. These became the 'Palestinian' refugees. They lost their homes for two main reasons. Some were driven out by the Jewish (Israeli) army and others fled after being told to do so by Arab army commanders, expecting an eventual victory (i.e. Jews driven out of the land), at which time people could return to their homes. Apart from extremists on either side, people generally accept these as the main reasons, though the proportions (i.e. what percentage were driven out or told to leave) would vary wildly, depending on your viewpoint. The Palestinian website, http://muslimwiki.com/mw/index.php/Palestine concedes that *"about half probably left out of fear and panic ..."*, which is a grudging concession to the Jewish view. The quote continues "... *while the rest were forced out to make room for Jewish immigrants from Europe and from the Arab world*". This leads us to examine the second refugee situation, the lesser-known and the largest one.

Up until 1948, Jews had lived in most of the Arab Muslim countries of the Middle East. In most cases they had been there for over 1000 years before Islam even existed. From 1947 hundreds of Jews in Arab lands were massacred in government-organized rioting, leaving thousands injured and millions of dollars in Jewish property destroyed. In 1948 Jews were forcibly ejected from Iraq, Egypt, Libya, Syria, Lebanon, Yemen, Tunisia, Morocco and Algeria, who confiscated property from the fleeing Jews worth tens of billions in today's dollars. Of the 820,000 Jewish refugees created by this situation, 590,000 were absorbed by Israel.

Now we get to the real point of this article. All the facts presented so far are from an endlessly contested history. People have argued about these facts until the cows come home and have got nowhere in the process. So I'm now going to ask you to move on from the murkiness of endless debate and into the light of certainties.

And the certainty is as clear-cut as they come. You can witness it with your very eyes. It is a fact that cannot be contested. Palestinian refugees still exist, in camps, on the West Bank, in Lebanon and elsewhere. Have you ever wondered why?

The 820,000 Jewish refugees who were forcibly ejected from Arab countries where they had often lived for thousands of years were all welcomed and integrated into Israel or the Jewish world elsewhere. There are no Jewish refugee camps.

The 750,000 Arab refugees who were displaced in 1948, were

placed into squalid refugee camps by fellow Arabs who had just gone to war (and lost) on their behalf but were unwilling to pay for the consequences. Incredibly, over 60 years later, over a million of these poor people are still in these camps, despite billions of dollars of relief paid by rich Arab states, the United Nations, the EU and others. Where on earth has this money gone and why on earth are they still in camps and not integrated into Arab society?

Palestinian Arabs are no doubt a peaceful, welcoming and gifted people, but they have been the greatest victims of the whole sorry affair, pawns in a wider struggle orchestrated by their powerful Arab brethren. For reasons known only to their political and religious masters they have lived for two or three generations within the bounds of these camps. Isn't a refugee camp meant to be a temporary home, as it has been for millions of refugees in other situations, until the people can be relocated to homes of their own? Not so here.

Palestinians were never allowed to be "ordinary" refugees. They have been kept in a form of forced captivity for a sinister purpose. A purpose that has succeeded in transforming a peace-loving gentle people into terrorist pariahs and has provided an atmosphere where it is considered holy and noble to send your children out as living weapons of destruction to blow up other children. Let's be honest here and consider who is really responsible for this tragedy. It is not Israel. Can't they see who their real enemy is?

"But they lost their homeland," you may say. This is true, though, as I have suggested, many would have been recent immigrants to the land, rather than having lived there for generations, as suggested by the propaganda. And, of course, they were surrounded by oil-rich neighbours who shared their race, culture and religion. A homeland in Jordan, for example, would have been perfectly possible and logical. But let's look at it in a wider context. Quoting from Encyclopaedia Britannica,

"The Russian Revolution of 1917 and the postrevolutionary civil war (1917-21) caused the exodus of 1,500,000 opponents of communism. Between 1915 and 1923 over 1,000,000 Armenians left Turkish Asia Minor, and several hundred thousand Spanish Loyalists fled to France in the wake of the 1936-39 Spanish Civil War. When the People's Republic of China was established in 1949, more than 2,000,000 Chinese fled to Taiwan and to the British crown colony of Hong Kong. Between 1945 and 1961, the year that the communist regime erected the Berlin Wall (opened 1989), over 3,700,000 refugees from East Germany found asylum in West Germany ... The partition of the Indian subcontinent in 1947 resulted in the exchange of 18,000,000 Hindus from Pakistan and Muslims from India--the greatest population transfer in history. Some 8,000,000-10,000,000 persons were also temporarily made refugees by the creation of Bangladesh in 1971 ... During the 1980s and early '90s, the principal source of the world's refugees was Afghanistan, where the Afghan War (1978-92) caused more than 6,000,000 refugees to flee to the neighbouring countries of Pakistan and Iran. Iran also provided asylum for 1,400,000 Iraqi refugees who had been uprooted as a result of the Persian Gulf War (1990-91). The breakup of Yugoslavia, for example, displaced some 2,000,000 people by mid-1992."

Then, of course, the Jews themselves, over the last 3000 years, have been 'relocated' more times than you could count.

And what of the "West Bank" or the *occupied* West Bank, as it is more often known? It is true that Israel "occupied" the land, since gaining it as a result of the victory in the Six-Day War in 1967, but who did they occupy it from? Well, believe it or not, the West Bank itself was illegally seized by Jordan after 1948.

After doing so, they made it an area forbidden to Jews – can you imagine the fuss there would be if Israel adopted this same attitude with Arab settlers! So, who did Jordan take the West Bank from? Before 1948 the West Bank was part of the area administered by the British as part of the British Mandate. It didn't belong to them, they were just caretakers. Before that, the West Bank – called Judea and Samaria by the Jews - was just the eastern part of Palestine, occupied by whoever happened to live there, Jew or Arab. It was not land owned by any state, as Palestine was just a neglected province of the crumbling Ottoman Empire. So, in reality, the West Bank has not legally ever belonged to any State in modern history. So when Jewish settlers make their home there, they are doing so on land that has been legally bought, not seized from anyone else, whether a State or individuals.

The crisis in the Middle East is over a strip of land the size of Wales, a hoped-for safe haven for a people with historical links to the land going back over 4000 years, a people who have not, in truth, been welcome anywhere else in the world. The fact that this land is surrounded by over a dozen nations gripped by a religion characterized by military conquest and subjugation is one of those tragedies of history that make you realize that there's more than meets the eye in the affairs of man. Israel is surrounded by nations that hate it intensely because its very existence is an affront to their religion. And try as they might, with whatever tactics they have at their disposal – even if this includes the callous exploitation of a whole people, the Palestinians – they will do their best to "right" the situation. They have failed to date, but they won't give up. That is the nature of Islam. You only need to look at its historical record.

There is a massive deception in the world today. It goes like this: *If those stubborn and wicked Israelis give the stolen land back to the*

Palestinians, all other conflicts will also go away. Apparently the Muslim world would be so placated that their leaders would just down their arms and the world would be a friendlier, happier place. Here are a couple of quotes that put a halt to that particular delusion:

"Our aim is liberating all of Palestine from the River to the Sea." (Hamas leader, Khalid Mishal)

"When we come to power we shall not allow the Zionist regime to live a single moment," (Ramadan Abdallah Shallah, Leader of Islamic Jihad for Palestine)

Land for peace? You've got to be joking.

Israel has become the scapegoat of the world, a role quite familiar to its Jewish inhabitants. In the Gulf War they were at the receiving end of Scud missiles, the World Trade Centre outrage was blamed on them by the Arab World and the highly anti-Semitic Protocols of the Elders of Zion is a best seller among Egyptians, amongst others. And the West has bought into this idea, too, though it has often remained unspoken.

When it *is* spoken, the words used are, 'If you take away the *cause* of the Middle East conflict then the Muslims would stop hating us', meaning, 'Why doesn't Israel get its act together!' A demonstration in London against a war with Iraq, had as many slogans, displayed or chanted, concerning the Israel/Palestinian situation as there were concerning Iraq. If Tokyo were hit by an earthquake, I wonder how long it would be before the Jews were blamed?!

It is time the world woke up to these simple truths.

12 It was like a massive weight had lifted from my shoulders, a great torrent of sanity entering my befuddled brain. And all of this at the hand of my loving wife. How wonderful. I wander into the kitchen, to find her sitting quietly at the table, reading a book. She puts it down when I enter and smiles.

"Feeling better now, love?"

"I should say. It's all so much … clearer now."

I sit down opposite her, placing the booklet on the table.

"This … does … answer a lot of questions. But …"

I choose my words carefully.

"How do I know this is the truth? … I've been exposed to so much opinion over the last few days, most of it delivered … with great emotion …"

"And you and me … we don't really do … 'emotion' … do we?" she adds, perceptively.

"That's right … I just feel such an overload. Yet … this booklet … does stick to facts and there are references to be checked and it does try to show both sides … yet …"

"Only one side can represent the truth … or as close to it as you could possibly get."

"Right. What do your Book club people say?"

"Well, we had a good discussion. Of course, we didn't have the same exposure that you had to … other opinions … But we reached the same conclusion."

"Which is?"

"It all rings true … but it does bring up new questions …"

"Join the club, Dawn. So many questions … but … go on, don't let me interrupt ..."

"That's OK ... yes, questions ... and the biggie is this one ... Why?"

"Why?"

"Why is there such hatred for these people ... even after the horrors of the Holocaust? ... That's the one that really hit us."

"Yes."

"So ... we decided to go deeper. Hence this book."

She lifts it up so I could see the title. A small book with a strange illustration on the cover. *Zionion – why does the world obsess over Israel?* By the same author.

"Strange title" I say.

"Yes ... but it makes sense. This picture here is of an onion, with many layers. It shows the layers of hatred against Israel. Peel one off, and a new one appears ... and so on."

"Oh I see."

I pause and smile at my wife. A wave of warmth comes over me, a sense of a togetherness that I haven't felt for a long time. I smile at her.

"Educated by my wife. How marvellous. Team Courtney, that's what we are from now on ... investigators."

"Team Courtney", she beams. "I like it!"

Later that day I was back at the end-of-terrace with Mrs Martin. It was a follow-up appointment to do some measuring up. She is easy to talk to and more helpful than most of my clients, in that she had a firm vision of what she was looking for and was pleasantly responsive to my suggestions and tweaks. We had covered everything in around thirty minutes and she had disappeared into the kitchen to fetch the tea and biscuits. I waited in eager anticipation, as I had been on quite some journey since my last conversation with her and I was looking forward to further discussions.

She soon arrives with the refreshments and sits down next to me.

"Well, Mr Courtney. Did you see the rabbi?"

"I did and I must thank you, Mrs Martin, for recommending him. He certainly put his case forward very well."

"Yes, I'm glad. He's really been in the wars lately, since the latest flare-ups in Israel and Gaza. You saw the swastikas?"

"Oh yes. They had tried to scrub them away, but still visible. Who would do such a thing?"

"Well ... that's the point ... if you lined up the suspects ... you'd have quite some line."

"What do you mean?"

"The obvious candidates would be Muslim youths angry over Gaza but then ... so many others are so angry, for whatever reason ... and this is how they ... vent it, I suppose."

"But swastikas? How cruel is that ... perhaps worse than just slogans. Probably Neo-Nazis, Mrs Martin. They are still around now. It never really went away, as I've just read."

"Glad to see that you are still ..."

"... Yes, my investigations continue. My wife has actually joined me on this. I must say that was a pleasant surprise. Her Book club gave her a book, Zionion I think it was called, that looks at this hatred of Jews, antisemitism. The book actually mentions around a dozen excuses for hating the Jews. Can you believe it? Even some of their own people – fellow Jews – I saw some of that at the demonstration in Trafalgar Square. But I also read something else."

I stop, to gather myself. I really enjoy my conversations with this lady and don't want to sully it through clumsy words. So, I choose my words carefully.

"This book has a chapter on … Christians. Not people like you, Mrs Martin, but … other Christians. I really couldn't believe what I was reading …"

"Let me stop you there, Mr Courtney … by the way, my name is Phyllis … yours is Derek I believe … I think we have graduated to first names don't you think?"

"Yes, Phyllis, I agree … but go on …"

"Christian antisemitism is a real thing, Derek … and it's far bigger than you can imagine."

"Yes, the book says the same thing. Why would that be? Isn't a Christian … a Christian, if you know what I mean?"

"If only … Derek … I'm afraid even we Christians are prone to … error, misunderstandings, even …"

She pauses for quite some time, as if the word or words she is about to speak are alien and uncomfortable.

"Hatred … there I've said it. Hatred … and it really grieves me, Derek."

I am lost for words for a while.

"Your husband is Jewish?"

"Yes."

Tears are forming in her eyes, but she gathers herself together quickly and her next words are spoken with a surprising, and impressive, boldness.

"Despite it all ... despite the Church in this country not being able to rid itself of this hatred ... my husband, Simon ... found his ... Saviour ... Jesus. How about that then? It's not all bad news, Derek. Jesus is still able to reach people even if some of his followers ... get in the way!"

"You seem ..."

"Bitter?"

"Um, passionate is perhaps a better word, Phyllis. But I can see where it is coming from ... of course this leads to so many questions ..."

She considers this and then, it seems, has a sudden idea. She takes a notepad from the table and scribbles something down, tears off the page and gives it to me. I take it and read her words.

IS THERE FUDGE ON MARS?

I look at her and she looks back to me with a slight smirk.

"Mmm, Phyllis, you don't seem to be a person who would make jokes."

"Jokes? No, this is serious ... this is the name of a podcast I've been listening to recently."

"Is there fudge on Mars? The joy of eating chocolate? Astronomy? I'm confused."

"Yes, it is a strange name, but I suppose that they just want to be noticed. It in no way describes what they talk about, by the way. They are just three ordinary fellows about your age. They are Christians and they have interesting views and a really quirky way of expressing them. They have covered just about everything ... recently heard them chatting about death of all things ... Anyway, they are going to look at antisemitism in their next broadcast ... might be good for you to give them a listen."

"I think I will ... sounds interesting ... and ..."

"Quite timely?"

"Yes. Strange really."

"You may think so, Derek ... but not by my way of thinking."

She winks at me. I am a bit confused and just give her a reassuring smile. I then glance at my watch and realise that I am running later than I realised and so bid my goodbyes.

13 Here I am, sitting in a Costa Coffee, waiting for a fellow called Steve to arrive. I was early as ever and was pleased to see him arrive early too, about ten minutes after me, but a full ten minutes before our planned meeting. *Like minds*, I thought. Perhaps this was a good sign.

I stand up and we shake hands enthusiastically. He is a bit older than me and a lot more portly. He sports a fine head of white hair, with teeth to match, a sign that he, too, has gone the way of the dental implant.

"Don't take this the wrong way but ..."

"I look older than I sound?" he ventures, his teeth briefly dazzling me as he smiles.

"You said it ... I couldn't possibly!"

I knew then that we would get along. He was one of the three "Fudge on Mars" podcasters, the one whose brain I really wanted to explore. It was also helpful that he responded so quickly and graciously to my request for more details in my email and ... that he lived not too far away from me. He seemed a nice guy and very approachable – as did the other two – when I listened to their podcast earlier on "Jew hatred". I thought it cheeky at the time when I suggested a meeting, but it all worked out and here we are.

"So, Derek, you have questions?"

"Many ... though, if this makes sense, I don't think I know how to ask them. I'm not necessarily looking for facts and figures, but it's the big picture I need, if there is one."

"Oh yes, there is a big picture ... in fact they don't come much bigger."

"Let me get some drinks, Steve. What do you fancy?"

"Cappuccino for me, please. Just a small one, though I think that's a medium in Costaworld."

"Right you are."

I wander off and queue for the coffees, as he waits patiently. It didn't take too long and we soon carry on where we left off.

"The bigger big picture, then?" I say.

"Yes. But there are two ways of telling the story. It really depends on whom I am telling the story to."

He looks at me and taps his fingers on a serviette. He is examining me.

"Tell me, Derek. Are you a religious man?"

I shrug. That simple gesture probably tells him all he needs to know.

"I see ... you'll get the watered-down version, then."

"Watered down? Why? I haven't got this far in my investigation to be fobbed off with 'second-hand goods'."

I meant this as a humorous observation, but perhaps it didn't come out that way. But he takes it well.

"OK, Derek, let me put it differently. Are you willing to allow your investigation to go ... wherever the evidence leads?"

An interesting choice of expression. It reminds me of the final remark of the rabbi a few days earlier, words that really chimed with me at the time. I stutter out the words.

"Y-yes ... I suppose."

"Then you get the 'full monty'."

I banish the immediate mental image of middle-aged male strippers from the film of the same name. Instead, I look at him with what I thought was a firm, determined expression.

"Then ... let's do it."

"Then, dear Derek. Let me tell you a story."

I lean back and sip my coffee and he begins.

"Let me take you back four thousand years ..."

He pauses to judge my reaction. There is none ... yet.

"To ... Bible times."

Again, he pauses, watching me closely.

"Are we OK, so far?" he asks.

"Just tell me the story and we can pull it apart afterwards," I suggest with a grin.

He nods and continues.

"It's what we call the Exodus, with Moses leading the Hebrew slaves out of Egypt, eventually to the 'Promised Land' ... modern day Israel of course ... a contentious idea with some today of course … anyway … back to the story. God had asked Moses and his leaders to meet him at the foot of a mountain and there asked them a question … do you agree to be My people, My representatives, My ambassadors for the world? … What do you think they answered, Derek?"

"Don't know … they agreed I suppose … you don't want to turn God down, do you?"

"Well you're right, they agreed. That's when they became His people … the 'chosen' people, you've heard that before … and … They agreed to do everything He asked."

He looks at me and asks a question.

"Now if you asked a Jew today the same question … in the light of history … what do you think they would answer … in fact, I'll rephrase that … What would be the response from ANYONE today about becoming God's special people … in the light of Jewish history?"

"The answer has to be … No way!"

"And why do you say that, Derek?"

"Because the Jews did not exactly have an easy ride, did they?"

"Right … and that … Derek … is antisemitism in a nutshell."

There is a pause while I take this all in. I try to summarise what I'd just heard.

"So, Steve. This is my perspective on this, as an outsider … an event occurred in the far-off past which made the Hebrews – and I suppose all Jews who came after them – believe that they had a special relationship with the cosmos, or God or whatever. And because they believed it, everyone else became jealous of this and lashed out at them … even if …"

I'm not sure if I had gone too far with this.

"... it may not have even been true, perhaps just a myth. It was just that they believed in it and, sadly, so did their persecutors ..."

Steve is silent as he mulls this over.

"And that is my take on it."

Steve responds.

"Mmm, interesting. Always good to get a view from the ... outside. Now let me play ... I suppose ... God's advocate ... hear me out, then we can discuss."

He continues.

"This was a *major* event, more significant than people realise, even some Christians ... This was the moment when a people ... the Jews ... cemented themselves to their Creator. A one-time event that was to have ... consequences. God had commissioned a willing people to be *His representatives on earth,* from this time onwards. Can I continue?"

I nod. He continues.

"Now we stand at the other end of history looking backwards. What do we see? We see a fractured world, with conflict after conflict ... we see the rise and fall of Empires, we see the conquerors and the conquered ... And all this time we have the continued presence of one people, the only people who can claim a continued presence in this world since those early Bible times. *The Jews.* Don't you find it strange?"

"You sure about that?"

"Oh yes ... ask the anthropologists. The Jews are the only people to remain intact as a people since those early days. They've seen everyone else off ... the Assyrians, Babylonians,

Hittites ..."

"Really?"

"Yes it's as if ... and you may not like this ..."

He pauses with a slight smile.

"It's as if they are being ... preserved. And ..."

"This I will leave you with, Derek ... How does this explain the hatred? A hatred that is like a 'many-headed hydra'. A hatred that has manifested in religion, politics, education, the media ... everywhere there are people, there is Jew hatred ... antisemitism ... you saw it at that demonstration – those people who are so consumed by hate that they are willing to believe a lie just to justify it! ... hate is the enemy of truth! Think hard, Derek, is it, as you seem to think, just jealousy ... or is there something more going on?"

At that he gets up, shakes my hand and makes a swift exit, after making one final remark.

"We'll meet again, Derek."

14 Dawn and I are sitting in the lounge, steaming cups of hot chocolate in our hands. She had downloaded a short anonymous piece from the Internet, which she had printed out.

God does not mess about. If He is going to commission a people to be His representatives throughout history, He is also going to ensure their survival, at whatever costs. And what a cost it has been, what a responsibility it has been, to survive despite the most relentless campaign of persecution ever endured by any people ever. Ask any historian, whatever their worldview. Antisemitism simply cannot be explained by them because, to understand this hatred you are going to have to accept what to some people, even many Christians, is unthinkable - that the Jews have been given a Divine mandate. They were chosen and are still chosen and this is not, for most of them, a badge of pride or self-congratulations, it is a burden that must be reluctantly endured by most Jews, who would gladly rather sink into welcome obscurity.

"I think this is what 'podcast Steve' was trying to tell me. He didn't give any reasons for this antisemitism. I think he wants me to figure it out for myself."

"And have you, love?"

"Not a clue, Dawn. Not a clue. How about you?"

"Even more so. Just one thing comes to mind ... there's a lot going on out there that we seemed to have missed."

"You mean about this Jewish business?"

"Not just that ... about everything."

"Why would you say that?"

"Well, you remember what you told me before about 'following the evidence' ... this book I've been reading for the Book Club is full of it."

"Of what?"

"Evidence."

"For what?"

"For things going on that ... more than meets the eye ... Look, here's an example. Did you know how much the United Nations hates the Nation of Israel? Here's a little snippet I picked up from somewhere."

She reads from a printout.

"Between 2006 and 2023 the United Nations Human Rights Council adopted not a single resolution against such human rights abusers as China, Pakistan and Saudi Arabia and has issued more condemnations on Israel than those for Iran, Syria and North Korea combined. It is also the only country in the world that has a standing agenda item keeping a watch on it! Why should Israel be singled out in this way? No prizes for guessing."

"Why would that be? Has Israel committed so many human rights violations?"

"Of course not ... that's the point. It's just another way to get at them. To say that China and those other countries are whiter than white ... look, I'm just a housewife and I can see a whitewash, especially when it hits you right between the eyes!"

I sit there, impressed. I raise my mug to her.

"Well said, old girl."

"Are you patronizing me?"

"No, of course not. I'm seriously impressed."

"We should have more of these kinds of discussions, love ... it's nice."

"Yes ... more than meets the eye, you said. What do you mean?"

"Well ... it's enough to make you want to believe in God."

I am shocked. These are not words I would have expected to hear from my wife. It is shocking, in a way, though I didn't really know why. Our married life has been full of the usual stuff; of family intrigues, holidays in Cornwall, illnesses and accidents, celebrations, weddings and deaths. But not ... God. He never had a look in. Both Dawn and I had not been raised in religious families, so there were no traditions to carry through into married life, no big questions to answer and no moral code to adhere to, apart from that furnished by our educational and legal systems. Why has God reared up now, attaching his wagons to a mild-mannered old couple who have done without him for decades, or even thought about his very existence?

Follow the evidence ... then act on it. What were we to do now?

15 So, we went to a Church. I just picked one at random, really. St James was an impressive old building that we pass every day on the way to the local shops. It was as good as any, so that Sunday, Dawn and I dressed in our 'Sunday best' (or so we thought, in fact standards seemed to have dropped with a prevalence of blue jeans). We were greeted at the door by forced grins and earnest handshakes. Leaflets were thrust into our hands, so that we could know who was on the flower rota, who would be speaking next week and who is poorly in the congregation, among other things. We sat in the pews, at the back, the end two seats. A Bible lay chest height and a kneeling cushion by our feet. Neither would be put into use in our case, I suspected. But who knows? The church was about half full, with around fifty people in all, dotted around, islands of the familiar separated by empty gaps in the pews.

Suddenly a bell rang and there was shuffling behind me. The minister and his assistant, all fully robed up, were arriving and everyone stood up. Even though a part of me insisted that I only stand for the National Anthem, I comply, not wanting to stand out (as well as stand up!) What followed was, I confess, a strange experience, not having lived through such a tapestry of song and ritual, apart from at the odd wedding and funeral. I could have been a visitor from Mars, for all the connection I had to these proceedings. Glancing over at Dawn, it looked like the experience wasn't quite so uncomfortable for her, there were times she even seemed to enjoy it!

The minister stands up to speak. To be honest, if you had asked me later to summarise his talk, all that would fill my mind would be the parallel mental journey I had lived through during that twenty minutes, summarising my recent journey. I had primed my mind for trigger words, such as Jew or Israel or Palestine, but none came up. There was just a vague memory of him talking about a man being attacked on the way to somewhere.

Afterwards, tea and coffee are served by the hatch at the back. I could see Dawn stride over there quite boldly and even striking up conversations. That was her thing and not mine. Instead, I wander over to the noticeboard, intrigued by a couple of posters pinned up there.

One is for an organization called *Christian Aid*. Its name suggests respectability, yet … all it speaks about, in terms of action points, is donating to what seemed to be Palestinian charities in Gaza and details about writing to your MP to complain about Israel's actions! The other poster is for *Embrace the Middle East*, again concentrating on Gaza and the need to send donations for the 'humanitarian crisis'. I look in vain for any emblems around the church that acknowledge anything of relevance to my investigation, but sadly find nothing. This was surely food for thought. From what I had learned so far over the last few weeks, Christianity was birthed from a Jewish environment and all of its early adopters, including the apostles and disciples, were Jewish. Surely there would be some acknowledgement? It was if an airbrush had swept through the building destroying all evidence of origins. All depictions of Jesus and the disciples, in the stained-glass windows and murals, were resplendent with halos and Latin slogans. How strange. I could see Dawn in an animated discussion with an elderly man, so I wander over.

She seems relieved to see me. She is also quite flustered.

"This gentleman …", she declares, almost spitting out the words, "… needs educating, Derek."

The man has a faint sneer on his face and I take an immediate dislike to him. I hadn't said a word to him but – judging by the effect he seems to be having on my dear wife – I uncharacteristically want to punch him in the mouth! I stay silent and let her talk.

"I asked him a simple question, 'What did he think about what was going on in the Middle East?' and he answered …"

The man butts in, not wanting to be quoted by another.

"… You mean the genocide that the Jews are conducting? It's disgraceful."

She nods to me and I join in.

"What do you mean, genocide?"

"Indiscriminate bombing of innocent women and children in Gaza of course. It's all over the papers. Surely you're not in agreement …?"

"This is a church, don't you think we should leave our politics behind? Isn't this meant to be God's house?"

"Yes … and God must be weeping at the actions of his … 'chosen people'."

I am determined to hold my ground and not to be sucked into politics and popular debate. I must say I am surprised that such conversations should be held in a church of all places. Should it be different here, isn't this meant to be a 'holy' place? So far, the past hour had shown me that, in everything I had observed here, there seemed to be no difference between Christians and the rest of the world out there. The other (frankly surprising) thing I have learnt was that … *this very idea really upset me.* I expected better. I had enough and, rather than being sucked into nonsense, I gesture to Dawn and we leave the building.

16   The next day I had yet another appointment with the dentist, an emergency one, as I had yet again damaged the fragile bridge in my mouth. Thankfully, I was only two weeks away from the permanent metal-reinforced bridge to be installed. The half-remembered joys of crunchy apples and chewy toffees were not far off!

Again, Dr Ahmed deals with me quickly. He had done this procedure so many times already that he had become extremely proficient at it. We had a chance for a brief conversation and, interestingly, he initiates it and, in fact, dominates it.

"I've been thinking, Mr Courtney … our little conversation last time."

I remain silent, partly because I was still adjusting to the new mend in my mouth.

"I felt that, perhaps, I wasn't very helpful to you, perhaps a bit defensive … These are emotional times and it is easy for us to get sucked in … we are just not encouraged … in fact positively discouraged … from having our own opinions and this is very true in my community, the Muslim community … perhaps I should go on a journey too?"

I let him continue.

"We really need to find things out for ourselves and I commend you on your honest investigation. What really impresses me, Mr Courtney, is that you have no axe to grind, you are not ... so to speak ... working backwards from the answer that you desire and that you are ... following the evidence."

This draws my attention. That phrase just keeps coming up. Why would that be? That strange tingling returned and I don't think it was the anaesthetic!

I had another appointment scheduled that afternoon with Mrs Martin. It was to make further plans for the work to be done in her house and to discuss budgets and such things. I arrived, mulling over my recent interactions, amused and slightly concerned that my conversation with the Muslim fared so much better than the one with the Christian at St James church.

Soon we were in conversation over the customary tea and, this time, delicious home-made cake. Apparently, she had baked it just for this occasion and I was touched by her thoughtfulness. Phyllis was now in my 'circle of trust' and I told her of my adventures since we last met. She was particularly concerned by my experiences at the Church.

"That's not on but ... sad to say ... quite typical," she says.

"Why would that be?" I ask.

"I'm afraid that most Church people are no different to all the others ... they just don't 'get' Israel."

"How can that be?"

"It's always been that way. More so now though, particularly in Britain."

"I'm confused ... but it does make sense with what I heard and saw in that church."

Phyllis pours out the tea and cuts the cake, offering me a slice (it was soft enough not to compromise my pesky teeth).

"But not all churches are like that. Ours certainly isn't. We respect the Jewish people."

"That's good to hear because … otherwise I'm tempted to just give up. If the Church doesn't 'get' the Jewish people, what chance is there that the world would … that's just not right. What do you think the reason is, Phyllis?"

"Well. On the surface … bad theology. Though I'm not qualified enough to say any more on that score. And …"

She pauses to gather her thoughts.

"Antisemitism."

I am shocked.

"In the church?"

"Yes, and I believe you saw it first-hand."

"But why?"

We were interrupted by a sound outside. It was a key in the lock of the front door.

"Simon's here", she exclaims. "He said he'd try and get back early."

"Why?"

"To meet you of course, Derek."

A slim, neat man enters the room, his arm already outstretched to greet me.

"Derek, I believe. Welcome to my humble abode … perhaps not so much humble once you and my wife have hatched your plans."

I am momentarily confused, until I realise he was talking about the official reason for this visit.

"Yes, Simon ... it is Simon? ..."

He nods.

"... your wife is very clear about her needs."

"Yes indeed, a very capable woman, my Phyllis. I leave this sort of thing up to her. My talents lie elsewhere."

"Yes, Simon is not very practical ... his talents are with the pen," Phyllis adds.

"Well, keyboard really, these days."

"Yes, of course. Anyway, Simon, you're just in time to answer Derek's question ... go on, Derek, ask him."

I think for a bit, to remind myself.

"Yes, Simon, it's this ... why does the Church here have problems with Israel ... and the Jews, of course?"

"What a question. What a question! Can I sit down first?"

He says this with a smile. I can tell that this was really 'up his alley.' He sits down and Phyllis gives him a fizzy drink, which he sips and then speaks.

"The Church and Israel ... the Church and Israel! ... You'd think they'd get on, no?"

"But look at it this way", he continues. "If the Church is the Bride of Christ – as scripture tells us – and Christ is God's son – as it also tells us and ... the Jews are 'married' to God like a wife to a husband, through their covenant with him ... what does that make the Jews to the Church?"

I am puzzled and try to figure it out but give up. He watches me excitedly, then intervenes.

"Mother-in-law of course! The Jews are the Church's mother-in-law! No wonder they don't get on."

I try a brief smile. Phyllis shows him her 'angry wife face' as if to say, *can't you be serious for once?*

"OK. OK. Jokes aside, this is serious business, Derek, and it goes right back to the early Christians nearly two thousand years ago who thought that God had rejected the Jews, His people and so they were to be persecuted for ever and ever ..."

He pauses then takes a Bible from his side table, flicking through the pages.

"Are you a religious man, Derek?" he asks.

This is the second time I had been asked this question, the first by 'podcast Steve'. This time I am a bit more prepared and I've had more time to consider.

"Well, Simon" I say, "If my only exposure to Christians had been the church I'd just visited ..."

"Which one?" he asks.

"St James, Islington."

He thinks for a bit.

"That figures" he says. It seems that this church was known to him. I feel good about that, it had turned him into an ally.

I continue.

"If 'Church' is what I saw at St James then, I'm afraid, I think I'd give up before I'd started."

"Give up? Give up, what?"

"My search."

"Aha, so you are searching for God, then?"

"Well ... um ... It's actually ... I don't really know. My search started off investigating Israel and the Jews – your people – but I now realise that ... to be honest ... your people and God are really intertwined and perhaps I can't look at one without the other."

"Good answer, Derek and I respect that. And it leads me into a reading. It's from the Book of Jeremiah in the Old Testament. It speaks of how God really thinks about his people."

He starts reading the text.

'This is what the LORD says, he who appoints the sun to shine by day, who decrees the moon and stars to shine by night, who stirs up the sea so that its waves roar – the LORD Almighty is his name: "Only if these decrees vanish from my sight," declares the LORD, "will Israel ever cease being a nation before me." This is what the LORD says: "Only if the heavens above can be measured and the foundations of the earth below be searched out will I reject all the descendants of Israel because of all they have done," declares the LORD.'

He pauses to allow the words to sink in.

"Does that sound like a people rejected by God?"

"No."

"Doesn't that rather sound like a people whom God promises to preserve?"

"Yes, I suppose. I heard the same thing from this fellow Steve, from the podcast that Phyllis listens to. He mentioned that the Jews are the ONLY survivors from those times ... It certainly makes you think."

"Yes it does, Derek and I think you've still got a lot of thinking to do. I tell you what ..."

He wanders over to Phyllis and whispers something to her and she nods.

"How about you come to OUR Church this Sunday? Our little fellowship. We don't meet in a grand building, just a village hall but ... does it really matter?"

"That would be nice. Can I bring my wife?"

"Of course! Especially bring your wife! Let us show you what REAL Church should be like."

That intrigues me. Has he set himself up for a fall here? My investigation is finally going somewhere, I think. Or is it?

17 So here we are, Dawn and I, having breakfast, preparing ourselves for a visit to the Brook Lane Fellowship. We're buttering our toast when Dawn speaks.

"How do you feel about this, love?"

"Not sure. Do you think we're going too fast?"

"No idea. Are you having second thoughts about today?"

"No, of course not. Look ... this Jewish thing is getting to us already; we're already talking like Jews ... answering a question with another question ... No?"

We both laugh.

"No!" she answered, "Just one final question ... so where are we?"

"I don't know. I suppose the main thing is that we're together on this. I hear too much of marriages being ruined over religious arguments."

"Right. Never thought I'd ever see us in that category."

"Me too. It's quite exciting ... I think ... what do you think?"

"Yes."

Her face doesn't betray anything more. She has a dreamy expression as she gets up and takes our plates to the sink.

We arrived at the village hall ten minutes early, as usual. In a way I wanted to catch them unawares, to give them no time to put on their "church faces." There was no-one at the door to greet us, which I found quite refreshing and the whole place rattled in glorious disorder. This rankled with the ordered architect part of me but the part of me that was driving this new enterprise of discovery was quite pleased. Dawn was not so impressed, she preferred neatness and everything in its place, rather than chairs being thrown around, men with microphone leads in their mouths as they adjust controls and kids running around like it was a skating rink.

We find a couple of chairs in the corner of the room and sit down. Very soon a pleasant young lady wanders over, draws up a chair opposite us and speaks.

"Simon's friends?"

"Yes, Derek and Dawn," Dawn says.

"My name is Gloria," she responds, with a broad northern accent.

I nod a greeting. This is not a place for handshakes, I notice, either brief nods or full-on bearhugs. Thank goodness they were content with the former, with us. I was wrong, as a small lady, evidently Jewish because of her jewellery, clothing and manner, reached over and gave us industrial strength hugs as if we were old friends. This was, to be frank, culture shock and I made a mental note of the positioning of the front door.

There were many differences to St James. For a start the music here was provided by a small live band, complete with drums and violin, as well as guitars. At the other church there was just a piano, unseen and behind a screen. Here, formalities were at a minimum, with little liturgy, just the odd bit of chanting, some of it in a foreign tongue that I guessed was Hebrew. By contrast to St James, an Israeli flag was draped boldly on the back wall and, on the table at the front, a portable cross shared space with what looked like the chanukiah in Phyllis's house, but with fewer candle holders. The music alternated between lively and contemplative and both were accompanied by a small dance team of mostly women, who seemed to be sequence dancing but with a distinct Jewish flavour. Some of them had tambourines, others had ribbons and flags. It was all very interesting and entertaining … but was it relevant to my needs? I wasn't sure, though Dawn seemed to be thoroughly enjoying herself, she even danced to one of the numbers, failing to lift me out of my seat. There are limits, after all!

The service was decidedly longer than at St James and the talk was longer, delivered, believe it or not, by Simon himself, who was eloquent and, in terms of the subject he covered, it was as if he was speaking primarily to me, re-enforcing our brief discussion from the other day, but going further. He spoke from the Bible, of all of the promises that God had made to the Jewish people and there was great sadness when he reminded us that the vast majority of Jews seemed unaware of this, despite these promises being from their book, the Old Testament. He also spoke on how believing in Jesus, the Jewish messiah, should have been the most natural thing of all for Jews to embrace and it was a tragedy that the reason for their failure to do so was very much due to the attitude that the Church has had to the Jewish people. I made a mental note to find out more about this.

At the end of the service there were some notices. A big one concerned a 'vigil' that was going to be held next Saturday at Trafalgar Square in support of Israel and the Jewish people. There were great cheers and excitement when this came up and it amazed me to see that this came mainly from the non-Jews in the audience. It was heartening to see the heart that these people had for the Jewish people. Dawn nudged me and looked at me with an expression that suggested she had made a decision on our behalf. We were to go to the vigil, she had decided. I, of course, had difficult memories of my last visit to Trafalgar Square, so perhaps I needed to go, just to exorcise the demons of that bitter experience.

We meet up with Simon and Phyllis afterwards over coffee.

"That was some talk, Simon. Was it just for me?" I say.

"You flatter yourself, Derek. I had prepared that sermon weeks ago, but obviously ... it was one you needed to hear."

"I do have a question, though ... and ..."

I turn to Phyllis.

"... this one is for you, Phyllis ... how does a non-Jew like you find a love for the Jewish people, when everyone else, y'know ...?"

"Good question, glad you ask" she answers.

"It's by revelation, I believe."

"What do you mean?" asked Dawn, suddenly very interested.

"Hard to say ... it's like God touched me in a special way, He did something in my heart. It's very similar to when I first came to believe in Him, too."

"Tell me more, Phyllis." Dawn was intrigued.

"Like the pair of you I was on a search, an investigation. I had no religious background, in fact my folk were rabid atheists, the sort of people you saw at that demo, Derek. They gave me nothing, my journey into faith was solely my own. This may have been a good thing, too as I had no baggage to discard, no negative Church experiences to turn me away. The thing is ..."

We are listening to her intently. She has to make sure we were still with her.

".. I'm not going on too long here, am I ... you would tell me?"

"No, carry on, Phyllis. It's fascinating" I assure her. She continues.

"Well ... you see ... it's really not about Church, it's about Jesus. That church you went to, perhaps it worked for some people there. If Jesus is there in some way, then he could speak into their hearts, whatever the church was doing. The same with our church. There might be some things we do that you're unsure about and I get it, we're all different and all have different boxes to tick. But ... it's Jesus ... the Jewish Jesus we follow, not any structure built by man. There ... I've said enough now."

"You did well" says Simon, squeezing her hand, "You should be up the front preaching. You're better at it than me."

"Now you're being silly," she whispers, reddening a bit. We smile, to encourage her.

"So ... revelation, eh?" says Dawn, partly to herself. I look at her, unsure what to think or say.

Phyllis breaks the mood.

"So are you two going to the vigil?"

"Yes, we'll be there."

Dawn smiles. I haven't seen her look so contented for ages. I wonder if she sees the same in me.

18 We were on the train to Trafalgar Square. As before, there were many people around and it became clear which of them were coming to the vigil. Many Jewish faces, young and old, individuals and groups. Also others, perhaps Christians, or just curious onlookers and observers. No banners, just the occasional Israeli flag. No noisy slogans, just peaceful chatter. It was comforting and, in many ways, a privilege to be part of something like this. It felt positively heroic and I marvelled at the trajectory that my life (our lives) had followed since the incident with the flag in the Lake District.

We exited the station opposite the Square in bright sunshine. In the distance we could see the vigil forming, in front of the lions and behind a staged area, complete with an impressive PA system. Our eyes may have been to the front, but our ears were to the side and we became aware of a jarring sound on either side of us. It appears that we were to run the gauntlet, flanked by jostling police officers keeping an angry mob at bay. These were the same people from all of those weeks ago, with the same banners, slogans and unbridled hatred, especially as they knew that this was not to be their day and their movements were going to be severely restricted. I point them out to Dawn, who had gone very pale and frightened. I hold her close to me as we move forwards purposefully.

"Just keep moving, just don't look at them."

She didn't but I did. I am sure that I saw Rahima there at the front, locking eyes on me from within her burka, though it was hard to tell due to the clothing. The eyes were narrowed and angry and I immediately felt the greatest sorrow for her. Here was a young girl, evidently highly intelligent and driven, giving in to hatred, rather than sampling the joys that life could bring. I had done some research since last time and found out that this militant form of Islam that she evidently had bought into had its origins with an Egyptian Marxist scholar from the 1950s, a Sayyid Qutb, one of the founders of the Muslim Brotherhood. This helped to explain the strange and sinister love affair between the two surely incompatible ideologies. *Is she aware of this?* I wondered. Are any of them here aware of it? I wondered whether this hatred of the Jews had origins in Islam or in Marxism. Perhaps it was both, each feeding the other. What a thought. I cast these aside as I entered the sanctuary of the vigil, when all I could hear were Israeli folk melodies, rather than the harsh rasping of a mob.

The vigil began, would you believe, with a singing of the English national anthem and a beautiful wistful melody that everyone at least hummed to, which must have been Israel's anthem. I ask someone about this and they say it was called the *Hatikvah*, the hope, which seemed a very noble aspiration. There were speeches, from Jewish and Christian leaders, as well as one or two Israel-friendly politicians. There were also silent times of prayer, ironically accompanied by the distant hectoring of the mob, who were determined not to stay silent. With the vigil there was no chanting, hectoring or slogans and very few banners in sight. It finished without fuss after about ninety minutes and the crowd started to disperse, heavily marshalled by the police. We got speaking to a young family pushing a baby in a pushchair.

They were reminiscent of the young family I attempted to engage with at the previous demonstration, but they couldn't have been more different. They were articulate and pleasant with a good grasp of the current situation in the Middle East and the worldwide repercussions. This saddened them and made them fearful. Their kids' school had to have guards patrolling the perimeter, how sad was that. Above all, they just wanted peace. They had Muslim friends and had the freedom to talk openly with them. They were the silent majority, the people who, of course, we never get to hear from because they are not screaming and shouting. They were so pleased that two non-Jews had taken the bother of supporting them at the vigil and thanked us profusely as we parted company at the station.

The rally had been peaceful, the counter-demonstration, however, resulted in over thirty arrests and a policeman was injured when his horse was spiked by a penknife. What a contrast.

It had been quite a day! We were relaxing with our hot chocolate before bedtime, reflecting on the events earlier.

"What a world we live in," exclaims Dawn.

"Right. To think that we've sailed through life insulated from these kinds of realities. There's one thing reading about it or watching it on the TV, but to be there, experiencing it!"

We aren't referring to the vigil, but rather to the hateful reaction to it. This was still a bitter taste in our mouths and totally overwhelmed the positive vibes we'd had, being in that peaceful gathering, hearing stories about Jewish achievements and listening to rousing songs and poignant prayers. My main memory was the hatred I saw in the eyes of Rahima, if it was indeed her. Of course it could have been anyone, but it's the hatred I felt that would remain with me.

"Anyway" Dawn says. "We don't want to take the negatives to bed with us, do we?"

"No", I answer.

I take the moment to bring up something I've been mulling over ever since that Church service in the village hall.

"Dawn?"

"Yes?"

"I've been thinking ..."

I must seem very hesitant to Dawn, who becomes a little impatient.

"Come on. Spit it out!"

"OK ... Dawn ... where are you ... personally ... with this investigation of ours?"

"Oh ... well into it. It has been such a revelation finding out about things about Israel and the Jews and all that's been going on. All my life I had no idea ..."

"No, not that ..."

This time I really did hesitate.

"With God, I mean ... do you, y'know ... believe in God?"

This time she hesitates.

"What a question? A bit direct, but then ... we have been married for yonks, you have every right to ask me."

"And ..."

Again, a hesitation.

"Why are you asking?"

"Because ... in that hall ... I really sensed that you were ... taking it all in, going with it ... even enjoying it."

"Yes, you're right."

"And?"

"I'm still processing it ... these things are not to be rushed."

Ah, that was the 'old Dawn' breaking through there. The careful, considered, neat and tidy Dawn. It was, of course, to be expected. As someone said – can't remember who – we are all on our own paths.

I wondered what my path was.

19 Dawn and I were sitting in the Costa Coffee, nice and early of course, waiting for 'podcast Steve' to arrive for our second meeting. I hoped he wouldn't mind Dawn being there, but she was insistent. The thought that she would miss a chance to further her education was now ... unthinkable. She was hungry for knowledge and Steve was the chap to provide it. I was certainly more ready for him than I was the first time we met. It's amazing how far we had progressed in our understanding of the world and all of the important stuff, since then. He arrived moments later, also early. Introductions were made and coffees were lined up ... the battle had begun. His was the opening salvo.

"Let me tell you a story, I don't think you've heard before," he says. "The story is told of Frederick II of Prussia asking his doctor – a Christian - for a proof of the existence of God. The reply was immediate. Any ideas what it may be, eh?"

He is met by silence. He continues.

"'The Jews, your Majesty,' replied the good doctor."

He pauses, allowing us to take this in.

"Why on earth should this be? Any ideas?"

Again a silence, but then Dawn chips in.

"I think I get it … the fact that they were still around … despite everything thrown at them."

"Correct. Well done … I'm glad you've brought your wife along, Derek."

I smile. Dawn seems satisfied with herself.

"But … but … this brings up a whole new factor, one that I never got to when we spoke before, Derek. I didn't think you were ready for it at the time. The last thing I said to you then was something like this … We were talking about antisemitism and how people – clever people like politicians and historians – had no explanation for this hatred. You'd suggested that it was just jealousy, which was a fair answer, but …"

He pauses for dramatic effect.

"Not the real answer."

He definitely has our attention now.

"Let's return to King Fred of Prussia. The existence of the Jews has been put forwards as the proof of the existence of God. We can imagine King Fred asking a second question … now this is where the rubber hits the road …"

You could have heard a pin drop (apart from the din of the other customers of course).

"'Do you have proof for the existence of the devil?' he asked the good doctor. What do you think the answer to this one would be?"

This time I answer, immediately.

"Antisemitism. Hatred of the Jews."

"Well done, Derek."

He pauses for our reactions.

"The devil?" I say, "That's the first time that's come up in our investigation."

"Yet ... always there ... lurking," he adds.

"That's a lot to ..."

"Well, let me add something to the story. I think it will help."

"Thanks."

"I will start with a question and then I will answer it. Is that OK?"

"Of course."

"How have the Jews managed to survive so long *despite* being hated by so many people? That's the question, an obvious one really. The answer, for me, is equally obvious ... It uncovers a drama that has been unfolding for thousands of years, but is hidden from most. The drama is a classic conflict between good and evil, between two great powers that have been in opposition since time began. Follow the evidence ... remember, Derek ...?"

"Yes I do and I like to think ..."

He interrupts, evidently on a roll.

"If we concede this possibility, then perhaps the evidence can start to make sense. We can see that the reason that the Jews have survived so long is that a great power has been *protecting* them and that the reason that they have been hated for so long is that another great power has been *attacking* them. This provides us with an answer to our key question. The reason the Jews have managed to survive so long despite being hated by so many people is because the power that is protecting them is *greater* than the power that has been attacking them. God against Satan, the devil. No contest."

He looks at us both and shrugs his shoulders.

"And that's that ... what d'you think?"

I ponder for a bit.

"It makes sense in a way that ... I suppose ... would have been entirely unacceptable to me just a few weeks ago."

"What a journey we have been on, love", adds Dawn, "and I'm prepared to accept that explanation, I think."

"So the good doctor replied ... 'Antisemitism, your majesty - hatred of the Jews."

Immediately the image of Rahima flashes before me, the hatred in her eyes. Where did that hatred come from? And she wasn't alone, it was like this whole group of, perhaps, otherwise sensible people, being sucked into this cauldron of hatred. Where did it come from? Perhaps it is as Steve says. He speaks again.

"The question that we asked - how have the Jews managed to survive for so long despite being hated by so many people? – cannot be answered by referring to the wisdom of historians, philosophers, psychologists, politicians or sociologists. They have all failed ... there is only one solution, a *spiritual* one, but, in our materialistic way of peering at the world, it's probably the last thing we want to hear. It goes against the grain of our secular world-system, but that doesn't make it any less true."

He carries on, like a politician desperate to get his message out while he has an attentive audience. I'm not sure, but his voice may have increased slightly in pitch, certainly in volume. So much so that there are now the occasional glances from adjoining tables.

"The truth is so plain to see that we should be shouting it from the treetops. There is an awesome, unseen battle going on for our hearts and minds. It's a battle that will continue long after we die and ... this is going to affect all of us regardless of whether we believe in God or the devil or whatever."

He stops. Perhaps he suddenly notices that he is making a scene, or perhaps he feels he has said enough.

"Any questions?"

Dawn and I look at each other. It is clear that we had one or two. I begin speaking.

"So, this Devil ... why is he doing all of this? Remind me."

"Because he hates God ... simple really!"

"Why?"

"Well that's a whole different story. Perhaps, for now, just accept it. It's not that I can't explain it, it's just that – on the journey you're on – you're not ready for it ..."

"Are you sure?"

"Yes."

"How?"

"I just know."

Dawn could sense a slight tension, so she decides to join the fray.

"So ... let's see if an ordinary housewife has followed so far ..."

Steve and I smile. There's probably some kind of veiled feminist insult there, but we didn't mind. She continues.

"God has this enemy ... the devil. Yes I can see that ... Who hates him ... for reasons not yet explained ... yes I can live with that. Of course, if I hated someone to that degree and saw him gathering together a group of followers, thousands of them, and declaring them 'his people forever' ... then I'm going to be more than a little miffed ... so ... it makes sense that the devil would hate the Jews and do all that he can to make their lives miserable because .... If he can't get to the Big Man ... then why not concentrate on the followers. Classic bullying behaviour, I reckon!"

Steve jumps to his feet and reaches over to hug her.

"In a nutshell ... put us to shame, eh, Derek."

I am both proud and upset, but smile anyway. Steve continues.

"And this ... has been played out in history again and again ... historians call it 'the longest hatred'. We'd thought we'd seen the worst of it at the Holocaust. Everyone thought that it couldn't get worse and 'Never again' became the slogan but now ... let me tell you a bit about our podcast. Yes, we call it 'Is there fudge on Mars?' A bit weird, I know, but that's the way we've progressed since we started. We cover just about everything and our approach is quirky, approachable we think ..."

Dawn nods in agreement and puts a thumb up.

"... but the origins were in our reaction to the horrors of October 7th, a little slice of Nazi Germany there on our 'doorsteps' so to speak. We felt that we needed to speak about it and other serious issues. The original title of our podcast was 'Now Everything Changes' ..."

"Now Everything Changes? I get that." I say. "It does, looking back, seem to have been a trigger point ... the world definitely has changed since then ... for the worse."

"Yes ... for the worse. And the biggest lesson we have learnt is this ... antisemitism has not gone away. People had thought it was a relic of the past. There were hints that it wasn't with Jeremy Corbyn and his rantings … but let's not go there."

The mood has definitely darkened. This isn't Steve's intention, so he changes tack.

"Look, folks. Let's stop focusing on the … bad stuff, shall we?"

"So, what shall we talk about?" I ask.

"God."

A silence, while I try to come up with something witty.

"Ah, the elephant in the room."

A poor choice of words I suppose, and they both ignore me.

"Any questions? Dawn, you must be full of them", Steve says.

"Mmm. You've caught me on the hop, Steve. A question? Well … how about … why can't God do a better job of it?"

"Now that's a direct question. I suppose you're saying, that, as the all-powerful God, why has He allowed this to continue? The antisemitism … the Holocaust … October 7th?"

"Yes I suppose I am."

"Nothing like a hard question to start with, eh? Just give me a few moments to collect my thoughts."

So, we did. He finally starts speaking.

"Why would a loving God allow the Holocaust? … Well … God could have chosen to protect his 'chosen people' I suppose … and he would be perfectly capable of doing so … the issue is free will … one of the greatest gifts God has given us … the ability to make our own decisions … of course, not something you see out in the streets at those demos, where people are acting on decisions made by others, rather than exercising this God-given gift."

"So, we all have free-will?"

"Yes ... to love ... or to hate ..."

Again I see the image of Rahima in my mind's eye.

"... to accept God ... or to reject him ... He could have made us all robots, slaves to his whims but he chose not to ... Basically, He just wants to be loved ... as we all do ... and love has to be given freely. Of course this brings its own problems."

"Which are."

"We can also choose to hate."

There is a moment of silence. He continues.

"It says in the Scriptures, in Deuteronomy I think, 'choose life, so that you and your children may live and that you may love the LORD your God, listen to his voice, and hold fast to him."

"So," says Dawn.

"We have a decision to make?"

"As does everyone at some point in their lives I believe. But ... in your own time, mind. I'm not asking you to get on your knees and cry out to God ... though you can if you want."

He said that with a wink and didn't follow through. I must say I was expecting the whole 'spiel' now, the Christian hard sell, the steps to salvation or whatever, the repentance and turning away, all the stuff you read about. I couldn't believe that Dawn and I had somehow entered that particular narrative. I for one certainly wasn't ready for this. And, glancing over at Dawn, I could see that she wasn't either.

"Too fast, too fast," says Steve, suddenly. "Don't worry, I haven't trapped you here to give you the whole ... Bible bashing bit ... you are, after all, free to leave at anytime."

He winks and stands up.

"I tell you what. I'll go and fetch more coffees and we'll talk about whatever you want to talk about ... just like average Joes."

We nod and he walks off.

"Well, dear ... that got a bit intense!"

"Yes. All a bit fast for me. You know that I don't make snap decisions. Like to mull things over, to stir it around in my brain."

"Got you there. All good stuff though. But ... perhaps not for us, Dawn."

"No ... perhaps not."

20   It was very early on a chilly day when Dawn and I trudged away on the A590, the road leading out of Ulverston, our backpacks a little heavy, but buoyed by the sense of achievement in this brisk walk. We finally reached Hoad Lane and walked its full length, then started the ascent of the hill. We could see the John Barrow monument getting closer and closer, a target like that was like heavenly balm for our ageing legs. Interestingly it is actually a lighthouse, which seemed quite fitting to us, a beacon to light our path of discovery, though not literally of course. It was interesting to read in the guidebook that, when it was built in 1850 it was promptly struck by lightning! Was God displeased? What made me chuckle wasn't just the thought ... but the fact that I would have such thoughts at all. God hadn't figured in any way in my life before! But here I was, on some sort of divine odyssey!

Eventually we reached the top and we had full sight of the brow of Hoad Hill. The flagpole was there ... but no flag. This was an incredible relief, more than you can imagine. We sat down on the bench facing the flagpole and caught our breaths after our hard (for us) climb. The view was magnificent, right over to Morecambe Bay and beyond. Anything on this flagpole would certainly catch the attention, one of the facts that sparked my investigation. It seemed so long ago, a different time. It was as if our life had entered a new dispensation and the trigger was right here before us. We paused and marvelled at the scenery, including the town of Ulverston that lay before us in the valley below.

"So ... this is where it all began" says Dawn, stating the obvious but perhaps wanting to diminish any tension I may have been feeling.

She is right, I am feeling tense. Not sure why. Is it the last vestiges of my confused state when I saw that Palestinian flag and the unsavoury early journey to find some meaning behind it? Or was it something else? Perhaps it was because of something that, very soon, we were going to do. I think we were waiting for cues from each other because it was some time before either of us actually spoke.

I begin to think through the events of the past few weeks. The people who plant Palestinian flags are really nothing more than foot soldiers for the wrong side. The Gaza conflict, along with every other conflict centred on Israel since 1948, has been blown out of all proportions. Why would otherwise sensible people spend huge amounts of time demonstrating against Israel when the world is plagued with conflicts that dwarf it in terms of injustice and scale of death and destruction. To date I've been told that Syria has killed over 600,000 of its own people since its civil war started, but you see no acknowledgement of this on the streets ... or on hills in Cumbria. This convinces me of the rightness of my journey so far.

It was Dawn who breaks the silence.

"Are we ready?"

"As ready as we'll ever be. Let's do it."

I unzip my backpack. Dawn takes out the result of her recent labours and gently unfurls it. It is a Palestinian flag ... stitched to an Israeli flag ... stitched to a Union Jack. She lifts it up for me to see. I nod my approval.

"Good job, Dawn. To think, sailors on the Bay will be able to see your glorious stitchwork."

"If it stays intact ..."

"... until someone notices it and takes it down ..."

"... and perhaps goes on a journey of their own", I add.

We attach it to the flagpole, intertwining the cord that we had brought with us with what was already there. We then slowly hoist it to the top of the pole, glad that it was still too early in the morning for other visitors to witness our 'act of benign vandalism'. When it was at the top we secured it then stepped back and did a selfie, with the flag behind us and Morecambe Bay providing the backdrop. Then we just stood in silence for a while. I feel a slight sudden shiver. I look over to Dawn. She has her eyes closed. Is she praying? Perhaps one day I will ask her.

We were unsure why we had done what we did and we didn't even talk about it on the long walk back. But we both felt, somehow, that it was the right thing to do. The idea of unity and togetherness is signified by those three flags stitched together. It may just have been a naïve gesture and not mean anything to anyone who may see it before it is inevitably taken down, but it meant something to us. It was closure, I think. But was it? Was it an ending … or a beginning?

As we trundled down the hill, greeted by the sweep of the flowery carpet, the birds chirped merrily away and the slight breeze caressed our faces. Nature cried out to us in a very understated English way, which perhaps summed us up to a tee. All we had done was follow the evidence … then act on it. All I wanted to think about now was returning back to our comfy semi and a glorious mug of hot chocolate before bedtime.

INTERMISSION

As we leave Derek and Dawn to chart the next chapter of their lives, the focus now moves to me and you. This is because their story is really our story, they inhabit a very real world and there really is a fine line between fact and fiction.

So, you are invited to join us as we delve deeper into the issues faced by Derek and Dawn because their issues are our issues too and perhaps a response is needed from all of us. What you are about to read may be difficult to process, but I believe it is essential. Everything really did change on October 7th 2023 and we need to understand the implications of this statement because we have already been affected by it and will continue to be.

We now travel back in time to 18th Century Europe, into the court of the King ...

PART TWO
The Jews, Your Majesty!

21 King Louis XIV of France and King Frederick the Great of Prussia may have lived in different places in slightly different time-frames but they are united by one historical episode, possibly an urban legend. Both were said to have asked either their Christian doctor (in the case of King Fred) or Blaise Pascal, the Christian philosopher, (in the case of King Louis) a single question:

Give me one single irrefutable proof of God.

The answer was the same in both cases, two words, *The Jews.*

Why would that be? We never hear the rest of the conversation. We too need to ask the same question and realise that the answer is not just the same, even after nearly three hundred years ... but more so!

This truth is going to be demonstrated, not through clever arguments but by observations, of the world around us now and the thrust of history ever since the Jewish people became an identifiable group. The clever arguments will hopefully flow from this and the evidence is going to be compelling, whatever your background or inclination. It is, quite possibly, going to turn your world upside down.

Now, we are all a mixed bunch. Some of you, like Derek earlier, will have no axe to grind, no stake in the argument, in which case I urge you to fully engage your mind and open your heart up to all possibilities. Others will be very divided on this subject, which perhaps already places us on the first rung of the chain of evidence surrounding this subject because there are some people out there with very strong feelings about the Jews without even necessarily having met one. This probably can't be said for any other people group. Some people think that every Jew is touched by God and only one step away from the angels. Others would say the complete opposite and declare them demons of the most heinous kind. Now, let's face it, this must strike you as odd, there must be even the tiniest impulse within your mind that's whispering (or possibly screaming), *what on earth is going on here?*

This section is written for the whole spectrum of the debate, because we surely all have a lot to learn, even if just out of academic interest. From the most enthusiastic philosemite to the most ardent antisemite, everyone is covered. So, this becomes a journey. You may want to leap aboard for the whole ride, or come and go as you please, though the former is preferred over the latter. Either way, we all have something to learn though, to some, it may be an uncomfortable truth.

The ship is about to leave. Hop on board now, it may be a bumpy ride.

22 We start with Gaza. Rest assured, we will not get into detailed politics and the varying opinions concerning the war. Enough has been written on this and all we need to do, in the context of this book, is to accept that there is a war, with positives and negatives thrown at both sides of the conflict. But I need to make a statement first, that this war and every other war fought between Arabs and Israel over the last hundred years have their origins way back in the past.

What interests me, at the outset, is the effect that Gaza has had on people. It has been extreme, more so in my view than any other conflict in my living memory. It prompted the writing of the first section, 'Derek's story' when a friend, David Jones, found a Palestinian flag flapping in the breeze on a hilltop in the Lake District, thousands of miles away from the conflict!

It has fed into the political climate of most Western countries, even affecting election results. It has resulted in thousands of university students in the USA and Europe identifying so much with the Gazans that many have actually 'converted' to Islam. I found this out through an investigation, not through a news report or YouTube video. I wanted to get inside the head of one of these students, so I picked, at random, a young female student at Columbia university in New York, who was taking part in the anti-Israel demonstrations. This lady was from a Christian background, as I saw from her Twitter (X) account, where she had posted a motto, *"Hearts are calmed only by the remembrance of God"* and she also pinned a post about the importance of Sundays, the Christian day of worship of course. So far so good and, of course, it can only get worse. And it did!

I then looked at her Twitter posts and it was interesting to see that, concerning the Gaza issue, they were mostly re-posts. This means that she was not posting anything original, just adding her agreement to the posts of others. This says a lot about the group-speak that drives this, in that original thought is a rare commodity. What I saw was so sad, especially coming from a "Christian." Here were some of the words and phrases she agreed to in describing Israel/Jews; "Nazis," "genocidal," "heartless evil demonic trash," "I hope they rot in hell" and "God's chosen psychopaths." She even posted triumphantly the fact that since the war started, 17000 people have become Muslims in France alone. Why would she do this? A troubling theme was developing.

She also praised multiple posts by an Imam who preaches on the "Muslim messiah to come" and also a post that declared that Iran was offering scholarships to students expelled from colleges for protesting against Israel. Is this not treason? In any other climate this would be a covert act, not boasted about on social media. But times are changing ... fast! I finally gave up on her when she displayed an image of the Hamas leaders, proclaiming *"The Good guys are winning."*

We should be saddened. We should be despairing, if this is typical behaviour of educated Generation Z, who will one day be in leadership roles in our countries. What we saw with this example, is a turning away from the foundations of the culture that nurtured her and her adopting an alternative mindset ... but for what reason? How can a political view prompt a person to actually adopt a different religion, simply because it is the one followed by the people group on whose behalf they are protesting? There is a curious connection between the Marxism of the far left – the driving force behind the protests – and Islam, despite the reality that, in their purest form, there cannot be any connection at all. A godless atheistic philosophy in bed with a theocratic religion? There is only one answer. *The enemy of my enemy is my friend.* So how can Israel and the Jews manage to become such an enemy of both, that it has drawn them together in a common hatred?

23 And this is where we properly start our journey. The actions of these students and activists and those who flock in their thousands to the regular pro-Palestinian marches all over the Western world do not actually, in the final analysis, have anything to do with the plight of the Palestinians. If they truly cared about the horrific

devastation suffered by the Gaza civilians then their banners would actually proclaim, *"Hamas, leave our people alone,"* because there's a simple formula to end hostilities. Just first give back the Israeli hostages and then lay down your arms. There's a crude parallel in many of the super-monsters blockbuster movies we love so much, such as Godzilla or King Kong, where the "monster" creates havoc and devastation simply because a human has either intentionally or unwittingly captured its babies/eggs and all it wants is to rescue its children. The havoc and devastation are just a by-product of this primeval need. The Israelis do not want to destroy Gaza and certainly are not targeting civilians, they just want their people back, held by terrorists hiding among the civilians. Give back the hostages for starters and it ends (hopefully).

There is an uncomfortable truth about the conduct of wars in our modern age. We saw it at Dresden, Hamburg, Hiroshima and Nagasaki during the Second World War. There are going to be civilian casualties. One mustn't forget that although war is often conducted by an evil elite within a country, they have been allowed to come to power, so the citizens of the country have to bear some responsibility. In the case of Hamas, they were voted in by the Palestinians in Gaza, many of whom were seen celebrating (and even taking part) in the atrocities on October 7th.

If the demonstrators' love for Palestinians is greater than their hatred for Jews then this is what should happen, this is what *true compassion* should insist on (not the least with the plight of the hostages themselves, many of whom have been killed in captivity). And, if this perceived love for the Palestinians was really coming from a place of compassion, then where are the demonstrations on behalf of the other 100+ armed conflicts going on currently in the world?

The Syrian civil war still continues, with numerous armed groups fighting each other and the government. Over 600,000 people (mostly Muslims) have already died in this conflict, dwarfing the Gaza casualty figures. Over 70,000 have already died as a result of the conflict between Afghanistan and Pakistan. Twelve African countries are currently experiencing war and little is spoken about the systematic targeting of the Christian community in Nigeria, where over 8,000 were killed in 2023. Pakistan and the Philippines are experiencing many armed conflicts, as are Mexico and Columbia. Then, also, of course, there is the continuing Russian invasion of Ukraine that the world's media seem to have got bored with, yet with casualties running in the tens of thousands. Yet the algorithms that control our news consumption seem to have overlooked these, none qualify for mass demonstrations in the great scheme of things. It is clear that there is a high degree of manipulation going on here, with some paths blocked by wrought iron gates but the road to Gaza open wide.

Unfortunately, there are factions within our society that are quite happy to inflame the emotions and peddle the narrative of hatred. Why can't people see this? Because hate gets in the way and it blinds us to reality. *And no hatred in this world is greater than hatred of Jews.* It has been this way for thousands of years and all these people are doing are sustaining this sad state of affairs. It almost sounds like a Netflix series, a worldwide conspiracy that spans the ages. Sometimes, truth can really be stranger than fiction and it is for you to decide whether to believe the evidence that will shortly be presented to you.

Thinking about this hatred, or any hatred really. Hatred has consequences ... not just for the hated, but for the haters too. At the deepest level, it's not a healthy state to be in. It diminishes you as a person, leads to anxiety, restlessness and paranoia and negatively impacts the nervous system, immune system and endocrine system. Simply put, it's not good for you! Then there are other consequences. When the current bubble bursts and truth can prevail in the current crisis, those caught up in the madness may find employment prospects severely affected and hateful social media outbursts coming back to bite you! Universities could lose financial backing from Jewish benefactors, who abound in the world of academia. Of course, they could compensate for this by accepting funds from 'other sources' such as Iran, which will bring problems of their own in the future. Academics who should know better would lose the trust of the system, their utterances and actions cemented into their permanent records. In summary, if you're going to succumb to the climate of group-hate, then you've got to be very certain that you understand the consequences. This is a warning to everyone. Think things through now before it is too late.

Hatred of the Jews specifically has often had negative consequences for the perpetrators. Over the last few decades many historians have endorsed the theory that Hitler could have won the war if he hadn't committed so many resources to the Holocaust. For instance, trains carrying fuel, food and ammunition to the troops were often allocated to transporting Jews to the death camps. His hatred for the Jews trumped everything and, ultimately, led to his downfall.

24 Then, most poignant of all, is the history of the Palestinian people that serves to provide us with the foundations for the current crisis. A key date was the 29th November 1947, when the United Nations proposed the Partition Plan for Palestine, a two-state solution,

with the creation of independent Arab and Jewish states, linked economically, with Jerusalem given special status. The Arab state would have 42% of the land mass, the Jewish state 56% (although much of this was the Negev desert considered unsuitable for agricultural or urban development), with 2% as the Jerusalem international zone. According to Wikipedia, *"Jewish organisations collaborated with the UN during the deliberations and the Palestinian Arab leadership boycotted it ... they announced their intention to take all necessary measures to prevent the implementation of the resolution."*

Fifty-seven nations voted. Naturally the Muslim countries - Egypt, Iran, Iraq, Lebanon, Pakistan, Saudi Arabia, Syria, Turkey, Yemen and Afghanistan - voted against the plan, not wanting any official declaration of a Jewish nation in their midst. Britain, to its shame considering its century-old relationship with the Jews, abstained, with wounded pride at its failure in the area. The biggest mystery concerned the attitude of Russia, which actually saw the Jewish Zionists, with their socialist leanings as potential allies in the Middle East. So Russia and its allies joined with Europe and most of the free world and voted for the partition plan. Without this unexpected support, the United Nations partition plan would never have been accepted, as it needed a two-thirds majority to be carried through. It was carried through, and the State of Israel was born into the international community.

May 14th,1948, was the date of the declaration of the State of Israel. A nation was born ... and immediately invaded. The war lasted over eight months, punctuated by the occasional truce. The Israeli victory was such that only a quick intervention by British delegates in the U.N. saved the Arabs from a more disastrous defeat. The war that was provoked by the Arabs to annihilate the new State of Israel not only brought a pride-thrashing defeat for them, but rewarded the Israelis with an increase of more than 40% of land, over and above that promised to them through the U.N. Partition Plan, including West Jerusalem! It was only due to the effectiveness of Sir John Glubb and his Arab Legion that the Israelis didn't take the whole of Jerusalem, including the Western ('Wailing') Wall, the holiest site in Judaism.

Let's stop and consider this. The Palestinian Arab leaders could have had a UN-sanctioned state in 1948 but, instead, decided to invade to grab the land by force. They failed and the result of this was the Palestinian refugee situation. This situation was brought about by a decision by the Arab leadership – not the Palestinian people – *their hatred for Jews trumped any desire for peace and co-existence.* Remember what I said earlier, regarding the current crisis, *if the demonstrators' love for Palestinians is greater than their hatred for Jews then Gaza would be saved.* Again, we see negative consequences for hatred against the Jews. Hitler ceasing the Final solution and the Arab leaders accepting the U.N. proposal; both would have enabled objectives to be reached if hatred hadn't prevailed.

The sorry saga continued. Again and again, the Arab leadership were offered peace proposals which would have given them a nation of their own. In July 2000, at Camp David, Israel PM Barak offered the most incredibly generous land concessions (almost all the Palestinians were asking for) in return for peace. It was rejected and, instead the Palestinians initiated a wave of violence (the al-Aqsa Intifada), in which 1,184 Israelis were murdered. In August 2005, all Israelis were evacuated from the Gaza strip, which was given over to the Palestinians. Two years later Hamas took over and we all know what happened next. There have been other initiatives since, in 2008 and 2019, all of which were rejected by the Palestinian leadership, who considered every suggestion a conspiracy and every initiative a trap. Palestinians will never know peace unless their leadership truly desire it.

Of course, those demonstrating for Gaza know none of this because it disrupts their "narrative," but any study of history would have shown them the emptiness of their slogans and the folly of their actions. One would think that University students would have been bright enough to study this, but hey ho! Incidentally I decided to visit one of their public demonstrations. Hearing that there was a permanent one outside University College London, I traipsed over there one morning to confront them (peacefully – it's the only way I know), only to find the place empty. Apparently, students don't do 'mornings! Quelle surprise! Not exactly a commitment to the cause that they are so passionate about, eh?

These demonstrators are actually doing nothing but harm to ordinary Palestinians. They are misrepresenting them, giving the world the idea that these are not peace-loving but are a people of hate, desiring nothing other than the destruction of Israel, *"From the River to the Sea."* The Palestinian people have become the world's pariahs to most fair-minded people, or even the 'less than fair' who are sick to their back teeth of the obtrusive protests and noise. In fact, perhaps ordinary Palestinians have more in common with Jews than they realise and this could be the basis for ground-level peace, rather than their continued suffering at the hands of their true enemies (their leaders and the Marxist activists). Believe it or not, and rarely reported, there are many Jews and Arab Palestinians who live in peace and harmony in communities all over Israel.

But there's another way of seeing Palestinians as pariahs, which is rarely reported. There is a historical record of animosity towards them by their Arab brethren in the Middle East, as we shall soon see. The blame for this should be placed fair and square at the feet of their own leadership since 1948.

The 750,000 Arab refugees who were displaced in 1948, were placed into squalid refugee camps by fellow Arabs. Incredibly, over 70 years later, well over a million of these poor people are still in these camps, despite billions of dollars of relief paid by rich Arab states, the United Nations, the EU and others. Where on earth has this money gone and why on earth are they still in camps and not integrated into Arab society?

Within these camps and other Palestinian towns and villages, seeds were sown, to ensure that the average Palestinian maintained a level of hatred for the Jews. It was (and is) implemented in their education system. A study commissioned by the European Union examined 156 Palestinian Authority textbooks and 16 teachers' guides. Eighteen texts are from 2020, the rest from 2017-2019. The report said they present *"ambivalent – sometimes hostile – attitudes towards Jews and the characteristics they attribute to the Jewish people"* and their *"frequent use of negative attributions in relation to the Jewish people...suggest a conscious perpetuation of anti-Jewish prejudice, especially when embedded in the current political context."* Examples include a religious studies textbook asking students to discuss the *"repeated attempts by the Jews to kill the prophet Muhammad"* and asking who are *"other enemies of Islam."* A maths text showed a picture of Palestinian kids hitting Israeli soldiers with slingshots to describe Newton's second law of motion. Terrorists are praised, and those killed are referred to as martyrs. Such references appear in science and maths books unrelated to the conflict with Israel. Also, most maps in the texts replace Israel with "Palestine."

But then, it is important to know the history of the Palestinians in relation to the rest of the Arab world. One fact we need to get straight is that *the Arab countries in the Middle East have no interest in a Palestinian state.* They would rather maintain the hatred (hence the school textbooks) and use it in their constant war against the Jewish people. The last thing they want is harmony and we must see this as a heartbreaking reality for the Palestinian people who surely, like every sensible person, including Israelis, just want to be able to live their lives in peace and security. And if you want proof of this, here are some verifiable facts:

The Palestinian refugee camps in Lebanon were taken over by armed organizations, from the Palestinian Liberation Organisation (PLO) to ISIS, including Hamas, the Popular Front, the Democratic Front and Salafist jihadist organizations. These groups acted against the surrounding Lebanese citizens, and in 1975 brought on a civil war that lasted for 14 long years of bloodshed and destruction. In 1970 in Jordan, the Palestinian terror organizations, led by PLO head Yasser Arafat, attempted to take over the country by establishing autonomous regions of their own in the north, complete with roadblocks and armed Palestinian Arabs who challenged the monarchy. In September 1970, known as "Black September," King Hussein decided he had had enough and would show them who was boss in Jordan. The war he declared against them cost thousands of lives on both sides. In 1990, Arafat supported Saddam Hussein's Iraqi invasion of Kuwait. In revenge, Kuwait, once it was freed of the Iraqi conquest, expelled some 400,000 Palestinians, most of whom had been living in the emirate for decades, leaving them destitute overnight. This led to an economic crisis for their families in the West Bank and Gaza, who had been receiving regular stipends from their relatives in Kuwait.

It's a sad tale and, if the truth is told, has its origin in just one overriding fact, hatred of the Jews.

25 Hatred of the Jews is not just an Arab Palestinian blight. In my small book, *Zionion*, I identified fourteen varieties of antisemitism. Here are some glimpses of a few of them:

The British government

The key political origins of the current conflict in the Middle East were the machinations of western politicians mainly from Britain. After the First World War the land was carved up by the British and the French, forming the artificial states of Iraq and Syria. Then, three-quarters of the land promised to the Jews by the British was taken away from them, giving birth to another artificial state, Jordan. Ever since Britain carved up the Middle East it has been cultivating relationships with the Arab ruling families, educating them at British colleges and Universities, such as Oxbridge and Sandhurst, leading to strong bonds with the upper classes and royal family. In the 1920s and leading up to the Second World War, Britain was given the mandate to rule the area of Palestine and its heavy-handed treatment of the Jews is well documented. Especially shameful was the Exodus incident in 1947, when a ship packed with Holocaust survivors was refused embarkation in Palestine and the survivors sent back to Europe, many ending up in Germany of all places. In recent times, in October 2014, the House of Commons voted overwhelmingly to recognise the Palestinian state. The fact that only 12 MPs voted against the motion was a telling one. Equally telling was the fact that the UK voted against Israel in a UN resolution on Jerusalem that referred to Israel as the "occupying power" and that Israeli laws concerning Jerusalem were illegal and null and void.

The United Nations

The attitude toward Israel is earthily summarised by a lowly Spanish interpreter in an unguarded garbled accidental broadcast during a session of the UN General Assembly in November 2013:

"I mean, I think when you have five statements, not five, like a total of ten resolutions on Israel and Palestine, there's gotta be something, c'est un peu trop, non? [It's a bit much, no?] I mean I know... There's other really bad shit happening [around the world], but no one says anything about the other stuff."

Her remarks were an observation that yet again the UN had convened to pass a series of resolutions condemning Israel, without a single resolution against not just Palestine but *any other global issue.*

There's a group within the United Nations that has become an enemy of the Jewish state. It is the *United Nations Human Rights Council* (UNHRC). It has 47 member states that each serve on the Council on a three-year term. To get quickly to the point I am just going to concentrate on those from the Asia/Middle East region. China and Saudi Arabia have served four times; Indonesia, Qatar and Pakistan have served three times; UAE, Jordan and Bahrain have served twice; Iraq has served once; Israel has never served. Apparently, in this region of the world, one's membership is in direct proportion to the scale of one's human rights offences. It's like putting a fox in charge of the chicken coop!

The situation is best summarised by a petition organised by *UN Watch,* with the following text: *"Contrary to the equality guarantee of the UN Charter, the UN General Assembly continues to single out* democratic Israel by 20 one-sided resolutions each year in the General Assembly—when murderous tyrannies Iran, Syria, and North Korea receive only one each. Likewise, at the UN's Human Rights Council, Israel is the only country in the world to be targeted under a special agenda item—at every meeting. Former UN chief Ban Ki-moon rightly condemned this act of bigotry. And this same council keeps a permanent investigator into "Israel's violations." Worse yet, the person they appointed to this post, Michael Lynk, swore that he was impartial, yet UN Watch revealed that he failed to disclose his board memberships on three partisan, pro-Palestinian organizations that lobby against Israel. It's time to stand up for justice and end the UN's obsession with targeting Israel with an endless amount of absurdly lopsided resolutions—while the real human rights violators instead get elected to high positions, such as Saudi Arabia's absurd election, by a 79% UN majority, to the UN Human Rights Council. I urge you and other world leaders to demand that the UN puts an end to this discrimination, as its own Charter rules and principles require."

The Media

There is a website called *HonestReporting*, set up to *defend Israel from media bias*. It is particularly scathing of the British media. They had this to say: *"The UK has been recognized as one of the globe's major centers of anti-Israel activity in the assault on Israel's legitimacy. This is reflected in the amount of material that HonestReporting continues to dedicate to the UK media, which is itself a major contributor to the hostile environment that has encouraged the demonization of Israel and BDS (Boycott, Divestment and Sanctions) campaigns. Media giants such as the BBC have a reach far beyond British shores while outlets such as The Guardian, which displays an outright hostility towards Israel, continue to gain ground with a substantial online readership in the USA. We launched our dedicated HR UK site in 2006 with an eye on the many British media outlets that have consistently shown an anti-Israel bias."*

The Activists

Israel must be shown to be an "apartheid state," based on racial segregation between Arabs and Jews. Jimmy Carter, US president in the 1970s, even used this inflammatory term in the title of his book, *Palestine: Peace not Apartheid*. So is Israel an *apartheid state?* Based on the definition of state-sponsored segregation between different people, as was the case in South Africa, this is simply not true for Israel. Here is a piece from the *Guardian* by someone not particularly known for his sympathies for Israel, yet ... *"There are few charges more grave. I should know: during 26 years as a journalist in South Africa I investigated and reported the evil that was apartheid. I saw Nelson Mandela secretly when he was underground, then popularly known as the Black Pimpernel, and I was the first non-family member to visit him in prison. I have now lived in Israel for 17 years, doing what I can to promote dialogue across lines of division. To an extent that I believe is rare, I straddle both societies. I know Israel today – and I knew apartheid up close. And put simply, there is no comparison between Israel and apartheid. The Arabs of Israel are full citizens. Crucially, they have the vote and Israeli Arab MPs sit in parliament. An Arab judge sits on the country's highest court; an Arab is chief surgeon at a leading hospital; an Arab commands a brigade of the Israeli army; others head university departments. Arab and Jewish babies are born in the same delivery rooms, attended by the same doctors and nurses, and mothers recover in adjoining beds. Jews and Arabs travel on the same trains, taxis and – yes – buses. Universities, theatres, cinemas, beaches and restaurants are open to all..."*

Academia

On April 6th, 2002, a couple of academics from the Open University decided that a response was needed to show displeasure at Israel's "violent oppression against the Palestinian people." It took the form of an open letter in the

Guardian, printed here: *"Despite widespread international condemnation for its policy of violent repression against the Palestinian people in the Occupied Territories, the Israeli government appears impervious to moral appeals from world leaders. The major potential source of effective criticism, the United States, seems reluctant to act. However, there are ways of exerting pressure from within Europe. Odd though it may appear, many national and European cultural and research institutions, including especially those funded from the EU and the European Science Foundation, regard Israel as a European state for the purposes of awarding grants and contracts. (No other Middle Eastern state is so regarded). Would it not therefore be timely if at both national and European level a moratorium was called upon any further such support unless and until Israel abide by UN resolutions and open serious peace negotiations with the Palestinians, along the lines proposed in many peace plans including most recently that sponsored by the Saudis and the Arab League."*

Thus began the beginning of the academic boycott of Israel in this country. Within three months 700 academics had signed up and words translated into actions when Professor Mona Baker of UMIST in Manchester decided to sack two Israeli academics from working on her journal for the sole reason of their country of origin. Three years later the *Association of University Teachers* voted to boycott two Israeli Universities on very shaky premises. This decision was later reversed after a huge backlash, partly prompted by the fact that the initial vote was made purposely at Passover time, to ensure a low Jewish attendance and that the decision wasn't thoroughly debated 'through lack of time allocated.'

A letter to the *Guardian* from Paul Miller a few years ago put the absurdity of the situation most succinctly (leaving aside the questionable premise):

"Israel's occupation of Palestinian land is intolerable but the academic boycott by the page of signatories is disturbing in its selectivity. China occupies Tibet, India occupies Kashmir, Turkey occupies Northern Cyprus and Russia occupies Crimea and eastern Ukraine. Moreover, many countries, such as Saudi Arabia and Egypt, have the most extreme abuses of human rights. In boycotting only the Jewish state those signatories evoke frightening memories of past boycotts of Jewish institutions."

Boycotters

According to Wikipedia there have only been six country-specific boycotts in recent history. If we ignore Nazi Germany, Cuba, apartheid South Africa and the mutual boycotting of Russia and Ukraine, there is only one country left, out of the Global family of 196 nations, and that is *Israel*. Quelle surprise!

The *National Union of Students* (NUS), in their online student guide ("filling you in on life and fun at uni!"), passed a vote *to boycott companies with Israeli sympathies, as well as products made in the country*. It "justifies" this action with the usual blanket statements, regarding settlements, Israel's military capacity and alleged human rights abuses. It also conceded that Nestle and Coca-Cola products would also need to be removed from campus, making sensible people wonder what connection this may have with human rights issues etc.

Then there are those involved in the entertainment industry, notably Roger Waters (Pink Floyd), Brian Eno (Roxy Music) and the violinist, Nigel Kennedy. Waters demands an artistic boycott of Israel until a list of conditions are met, including the right of return of all Palestinian refugees. In February 2015, 700 entertainers said they would boycott Israel until its "colonial oppression of Palestinians" ended, drawing parallels to apartheid-era South Africa.

The World Council of Churches joined the party in 2001,

followed by the Presbyterian Church in the USA, the United Church of Christ and the United Methodist Church. In 2009 the *Kairos Palestine document* was drawn up by Palestinian Christians, bringing God into the political arena and "assuring" the World that the "occupation" was a "sin against God."

All of these actions eventually found a point of focus in 2005 with the Palestinian-led *Boycott, Divestment and Sanctions movement* (BDS), which modelled itself on the anti-apartheid movement that opposed the racist regime in South Africa. They now self-declare as a "vibrant global movement made up of unions, academic associations, churches and grassroots movements across the world" and, to be consistent with our on-going narrative, stress the two prejudicial triggers of *apartheid* and *colonisation*.

Neo-Nazis

Here is the story in the UK. After laying low for nine years, neo-Naziism entered the public arena as the *League of Empire Loyalists* in 1954, a pressure group opposed to the dissolution of the British Empire and led by a leading fascist, Arthur Chesterton. Its core belief was that Russian Bolshevism and American-style Capitalism were actually working together as a Jewish conspiracy against the British Empire! This group led to the formation of the *British National Party* (BNP) in 1960. After some internal splits this group morphed into the *National Front* (NF) in 1967. This became the biggest far-right political party in the UK in the 1970s and gained a degree of acceptance in some working-class areas, even polling 44% in a local election in Deptford. This group soon declined in the 1980s and the *British National Party* re-emerged in 1982 and is still with us today.

When Nick Griffin took over the party he tried to water down the antisemitism promoted by the party. He said: "*we can get away with criticising Zionists, but any criticism of Jews is likely to be legal and political suicide."* A pragmatic statement, rather than a change of heart! In their literature, reference to Jews was obscured through the use of the term "Zionists" and there are various references to an unnamed "group of conspirators" who have worked against the nationalistic elements of British society and are even responsible for the *Islamification* of the country!

So, the old hatreds are still there, despite the testimony of history that shows the outcome of such hatreds. This is all swept under the carpet through the twisted viewpoint known as *Holocaust denial*. To try and normalise their hatreds, the best solution these people can produce to address the situation in Nazi Europe in the 1940s is to actually deny that it ever happened, despite the overwhelming evidence, not the least from survivors of the Holocaust. Holocaust denial is so insidious that it has been declared illegal in several countries, including Austria, Germany, Hungary and Romania that were perpetrators of the Holocaust. There have been numerous convictions of individuals who have fallen foul of these laws and have received hefty fines or imprisonment, including Jean-Marie Le Pen, father of the high-profile French politician, Marine Le Pen.

Conspiracy Buffs

The *Protocols of the Elders of Zion* is probably the most well-known weapon in the armoury of anti-Jewish conspiracy nuts. It is also a *complete forgery*, but why should the truth get in the way of a good yarn? It is claimed to be the minutes of a meeting of Jewish leaders at the first Zionist congress in Basel, Switzerland in 1897 (or, as some say, a graveyard in Prague), when the Jews were hatching an audacious plot to take over the world!

What it actually was is not that easy to follow. It seems to be based on a pamphlet written at the turn of the 20th Century by a Russian forger as a means to discredit reforms in that country and bolster the influence of the Czar. This forger took material from a satire on Napoleon III by Maurice Joly and from a novel by Hermann Goedesche, a 19th Century German antisemite. The final form of the Protocols first appeared in Russia in around 1905, becoming a best seller by 1920 and promoted in the USA by none other than Henry Ford, who when he wasn't building cars was ranting and raving about Jews. It was first exposed as a forgery by Philip Graves of *the Times* in 1921, but not before one Adolph Hitler had a chance to read it and believe it. Possibly after noticing that car sales were plummeting in parts of New York, Henry Ford was forced to make a public retraction, admitting that the book that he wrote in 1920, *The International Jew,* was based on the Protocols.

Most of the other so-called Jewish conspiracies are simply variations on the theme or *strategies* to achieve world domination over the last few hundred years. Let's summarise a few of them:

- in 1775 Jews financed the American Revolution.

- in 1933 Jews conspired against the Germans and caused World War II.

- in 1990 Jews conspired against the Iraqis and caused the Gulf War.

- in 1999 Jews conspired to incite the bombing of Serbs in Serbia.

- in 2001 Jews were the real instigators of 9-11.

- Jews have instigated, supported and financed World War I, the Cold War, the Korean War, the Vietnam War as part of a perpetual Jewish war against the rest of the World.

26 What a story! This should be shouted from the rooftops, yet what I have shown you is just a small glimpse into a vast sea of prejudice.

Now that you have seen that antisemitism, hatred of the Jews, is not just an Israel/Palestinian thing we are left with the uncomfortable question, which is this; *what on earth is it then?* We have reached an uncomfortable truth, that the World, for whatever reason, just doesn't like Jews. They may veil their hatred by directing their ire towards Israel or Zionism, but it's all the same, just antisemitism dressed differently. The key words here are "for whatever reason" and it is these words that are going to lead us deeper into the heart of this problem.

For whatever reason? In the story of Moses and the Exodus, the Egyptian Pharaoh thought he had a reason; *they may grow too large and turn against us.*

For whatever reason? The Church fathers thought they had a reason; *after all the Jews killed Christ, didn't they?*

For whatever reason? In the early days of the Church, Roman emperor Constantine thought he had a reason; *they were encouraging Christianity to remain too Jewish.*

For whatever reason? The medieval Church thought it had a reason; *they stole communion wafers in order to stick pins in them and trample on them, so torturing Christ!*

For whatever reason? The Protestant leader, Martin Luther, thought he had a reason after many years of trying to convince the Jews; *they refused to convert to Christianity!*

For whatever reason? French rationalist philosopher Voltaire thought he had a reason; *they gave us Christianity!*

For whatever reason? The Nazis and neo-Nazis thought they had a reason; *they are an inferior race!*

For whatever reason? The Palestinians think they have a reason; *they have stolen our land!*

For whatever reason? The United Nations, the activists, boycotters, academics and others think they have a reason; *their country is probably the most evil nation in the World!*

There's an awful lot of "for whatever reasons" and I haven't even started on those who blame the Jews for capitalism, communism, 9-11, the two World Wars, polluting the Aryan race, Hollywood (we'll concede that one!) on a list that grows longer year by year. It's that word "whatever." It tells us that the world will *always* find a reason to hate Jews, it's an unescapable fact and it's unlikely to change any time soon. And, as history has shown us ... there are always *consequences.* Thoughts usually lead to actions and, although this has rarely been good news, there are people in this world who are not burdened by prejudice, who read the truth ... and act on it. Can you be one of these people? The best antidote to lies and prejudice is education in the truth. Hopefully this book has made a difference.

There has never been a satisfactory explanation for antisemitism from historians, philosophers, psychologists, sociologists, economists and social commentators, for the simple reason that it seems to be driven by *blind irrational hatred.* Can this really be orchestrated, the greatest conspiracy of all? Is this possible?

The central plotline for the old Sci-Fi film, *Quatermass and the Pit,* involves mankind comprising two competing races, one sporadically, at various times in history, emerging and purging the other in an act of ethnic cleansing. This could easily be a picture of the workings of antisemitism, re-inventing itself in every generation but following the same pattern of purging mankind of the 'others.'

So, when you see Palestinian flags and pro-Palestinian posters and banners everywhere, in High streets, University campuses and even Lake District beauty spots, it is not what it seems. It is nothing to do with sympathy for the Palestinians, but all to do with hatred for the Jews. It is not love and sympathy for a beleaguered people, but rather disregard and hatred of eternal pariahs in the world's eyes. Every flag, poster and banner may as well all say the same thing, 'We hate Jews,' or simply feature a single swastika, black on a white circle, with a red background. It could be a Nuremberg rally of the Nazi era, or the flags of the Roman legions as they sacked Jerusalem, or the red-crossed emblems of the Crusaders massacring Jews in their villages on the way to the "Holy Land." It is all the same, they all share the same spirit of evil.

It is the modern chapter of a historical 'danse macabre', where the unwitting actors are the activists, students, campaigners, Marxists and even those with no axe to grind but who have been told that this is the 'acceptable thing to do.' It's the same old story, redressed for modern times and those who have become actors in the drama will, one day, live to regret their actions once the penny has dropped. And it will not be good for their soul! At the recent Eurovision song contest, proudly displaying the motto, *united by music,* the only thing that seemed to unite the appointed juries was their distaste for Israel, reflected in their voting. No jury awarded Israel top marks and it got 52 points in total. This is not sour grapes as when the 'ordinary people' voted, Israel received the second highest total, of 323 after Croatia, which had 337. The officials voted with their virtue-signalling hats on, whereas people like you and I voted with their conscience and perhaps with sympathy for the battering Israel has received by those who run our world (and ridiculous song competitions – just my view, folks!) Perhaps there is a lot of fairness and decency out there, it's just that we rarely get a chance to see it! This brings us to an important point. Perhaps what we see here is a statement from the 'silent majority', albeit in a safe, anonymous way. A *protest against the protests*, in the name of fairness and decency perhaps?

It's not that caring for the plight of Palestinians is a bad thing, but let's not pretend that this is the real reason for the demonstrations, rallies, marches, sit-ins etc. It's not that Palestinians don't have legitimate claims to want to live in peace, but they are just one of a long line of displaced people throughout history. Reminding ourselves of the quote from Encyclopaedia Brittanica:

"The Russian Revolution of 1917 and the postrevolutionary civil war (1917-21) caused the exodus of 1,500,000 opponents of communism. Between 1915 and 1923 over 1,000,000 Armenians left Turkish Asia Minor, and several hundred thousand Spanish Loyalists fled to France in the wake of the 1936-39 Spanish Civil War. When the People's Republic of China was established in 1949, more than 2,000,000 Chinese fled to Taiwan and to the British crown colony of Hong Kong. Between 1945 and 1961, the year that the communist regime erected the Berlin Wall (opened 1989), over 3,700,000 refugees from East Germany found asylum in West Germany ... The partition of the Indian subcontinent in 1947 resulted in the exchange of 18,000,000 Hindus from Pakistan and Muslims from India--the greatest population transfer in history. Some 8,000,000-10,000,000 persons were also temporarily made refugees by the creation of Bangladesh in 1971 ... During the 1980s and early '90s, the principal source of the world's refugees was Afghanistan, where the Afghan War (1978-92) caused more than 6,000,000 refugees to flee to the neighbouring countries of Pakistan and Iran. Iran also provided asylum for 1,400,000 Iraqi refugees who had been uprooted as a result of the Persian Gulf War (1990-91). The

breakup of Yugoslavia, for example, displaced some 2,000,000 people by mid-1992."

We can now add to this list. Over 6.8 million people have fled the current conflict in Syria, out of around 27.1 million refugees in the world by the end of 2021. This includes 6.1 million from Afghanistan and 5.9 million from Ukraine. The Palestinian situation is totally dwarfed by these statistics and is totally orchestrated for political reasons. Where are the demonstrations and University sit-ins for the Afghans, Syrians or Ukrainians? And no people in the world have, ironically, been displaced more than … yes you guessed … the Jews themselves! For instance, if the descendants of Jews who were kicked out of England in 1290 put in a claim for the money that was stolen from them in the process by the English 'nobility', our country would probably be bankrupted.

27

Now put on your thinking cap. Do we think that the following can be explained by a series of co-incidences and anomalies of history?

That a single people can survive for over four thousand years as a distinct race despite being blamed and punished for killing their own Saviour (Jesus), corrupting Christians, host desecration (trampling on communion wafers), tampering with the currency, refusing to convert to Christianity, giving Christianity to the world, being an inferior race, stealing Palestinian land, apartheid, genocide, ethnic cleansing, child killing, being colonial conquerors, being in league with the devil, creating capitalism and communism, being behind 9-11, the two World Wars, polluting the Aryan race, the Black Death and, if that wasn't enough, *plotting to take over the world.*

Also …

That a single people group can survive for over four thousand years as a distinct race despite being insulted, persecuted, expelled, murdered, massacred and deemed worthy of genocide (by Nazis and Islamists).

Can you honestly believe that any of this makes sense? Unless something is going on beyond our capacity for reasoning and understanding. Either of the above lists is unbelievable enough but for a people to survive four thousand years despite all they have been blamed and punished for - including a systematic campaign of genocide by the Nazis that massacred almost a third of them – is beyond unbelievable if that were possible.

And, to add to this, while we're on a roll, *to actually thrive as a people. There are just over 15.7 million Jews world-wide (2023* figures), showing that about *0.2% of the world is Jewish* – about 1 person out of every 500. The expectation is that 0.2% of the world's scientists, musicians, entertainers and writers would, on average, be Jewish. Not so. Just looking at the period since the mid-19th Century we find that *about 25% of the world's scientists have been Jews* and that 22% of all Nobel Prize winners in the 20th Century were Jewish. Jewish people have impacted the world in so many different spheres and have influenced the thinking of the world dramatically; the three men who have, arguably, most influenced the 20th Century, Albert Einstein, Sigmund Freud and Karl Marx, were all Jewish, as were the founders of two of the main world religions, Judaism and Christianity.

It's the stuff of fiction or a good movie. Incidentally, if we just look at one area, the musical theatre, the following musicals were composed by Jews: *Fiddler on the Roof, Oliver, West Side Story, The Sound of Music, Show Boat, Porgy and Bess, South Pacific, The King and I, Annie Get your Gun, Cabaret, Camelot, Carousel, Chicago,*

A Chorus Line, Fame, 42nd Street, Funny Girl, Gigi, Godspell, Guys and Dolls, La Cage aux Folles, Les Miserables, A Little Night Music, Little Shop of Horrors, Mary Poppins, Miss Saigon, My Fair Lady, Oklahoma!, The Producers and *The Wizard of Oz.* It's harder to find one that *isn't* Jewish! The only major composer in the most prolific period (mid-20th Century) who wasn't Jewish was Cole Porter, who explained how he made the leap to Broadway theatres: *"I'll just write Jewish tunes."* Irving Berlin, one of the major songwriters of the 20th Century, was to write *White Christmas* (ironic, eh?), *Easter Parade* (even more ironic), *God Bless America* and *There's no Business like Show Business.* In 1924 it was remarked that *"Irving Berlin has no place in American music. He is American Music."*

Other lists can be made in virtually every sphere of human life and endeavour (except, perhaps, sports!)

28 There was one man who probably understood the Jew better than most Jews today understand themselves, in terms of what they represent and their accomplishments. His name was Adolph Hitler. He understood the uniqueness of the Jews as a people. He realized that Jews can never be successfully integrated with the rest of humanity and he made it his task to ensure that they never would be.

Hitler's form of antisemitism was not a means to an end; it was a goal in and of itself. The Nuremberg Laws, established in 1935, effectively destroyed the Jewish community of Germany - but this was not enough to satisfy Hitler. He saw the Jewish nation as his mortal enemy, and so they became his target for total destruction. He said, *"The struggle for world domination will be fought entirely between us - between Germans and Jews. All else is facade*

121

and illusion. Behind England stands Israel, and behind France, and behind the United States. Even when we have driven the Jew out of Germany, he remains our world enemy."

He famously said, *"Providence has ordained that I should be the greatest liberator of humanity. I am freeing man from the restraints of an intelligence that has taken charge, from the dirty and degrading self-mortifications of a false vision known as conscience and morality, and from the demands of a freedom and personal independence which only a very few can bear … The Ten Commandments have lost their vitality. Conscience is a Jewish invention; it is a blemish, like circumcision."*

This is worth unpacking, though it will take us into new areas, with a different perspective as to the origins of antisemitism. For some of you readers, this may be a point of departure, which is a shame and I do implore you to hang around. This is because we are now going to delve into the origins of this *longest hatred* and, having exhausted all natural explanations for it, confounding the historians, social scientists, psychologists, anthropologists, sociologists and anyone else with an 'ology,' we are now going to enter the realm of the *supernatural*. This is not 'X files' territory, but I am about to open my Bible. We are going to look at the origin story in the Christian Old Testament, aka the Hebrew Bible of the Jews themselves.

This is because Hitler declared that conscience and morality were a bad thing and that they were a *Jewish invention* and thereby giving us some clues as to why he hated them so much. He was right about them being a 'Jewish thing,' though of course he was wrong about them being a *bad thing*. Everything that is relevant to our story began about 4,000 years ago, at the foot of a mountain in the Sinai Desert. Reading from the 24th Chapter of Exodus:

"Then the LORD said to Moses, "Come up to the LORD, you and Aaron,

Nadab and Abihu, and seventy of the elders of Israel. You are to worship at a distance, but Moses alone is to approach the LORD; the others must not come near. And the people may not come up with him. When Moses went and told the people all the LORD's words and laws, they responded with one voice, "Everything the LORD has said we will do." Moses then wrote down everything the LORD had said."

Here's the scene. Moses led the Hebrews (the forefathers of the Jewish people) from their slavery at the hands of the Egyptian Pharaoh. They had miraculously crossed the Red Sea and now well over a million of them stand near the foot of Mount Sinai. Moses had climbed up and met with God, receiving many instructions and teachings. He now returns and tells the elders what he has learned. This is the basis of Hitler's objection because this was the 'giving of the Law' to Moses, then the Jewish people, then the world. This was the *Ten Commandments* that Hitler hated because they condemned just about everything he did, and a lot more. The Jewish people accepted these teachings, as it turned out, on behalf of you and me, saying, *everything the LORD has said we will do.* This, as it turned out, was the start of their troubles. In the next passage, we see this becoming a contract, or covenant, between them and God. It was *that* serious.

"This is the blood of the covenant that the LORD has made with you in accordance with all these words." (Exodus 24:1-8)

This was a *major* event, more significant than people realise, even many Christians. This was the moment when a people – represented by their leadership – cemented themselves to their Creator. This was a one-time event that was to have eternal consequences. God had commissioned a willing people to be *His representatives on Earth*, from this time onwards. Hold onto that thought.

Now we stand at the other end of history looking backwards. What do we see? We see a fractured world, riven by conflict after conflict, we see the rise and fall of Empires, we see the conquerors and the conquered, roles continually shifting as time progresses. The blood-soaked earth cries out, 'will this ever end?', knowing that all that we see acted out are physical manifestations of man's struggles against God and the perfect world He had created. And if a theme presents itself, it is the continued presence of *one people*, the only survivors of this eternal conflict, the only people who can claim a continued presence in this world since those early Bible times. *The Jews.* The inheritors of the promises made by Moses and his elders all of those centuries ago.

God does not mess about. If He is going to commission a people to be His representatives throughout history, He is also going to ensure their survival, at whatever costs. And what a cost it has been, what a responsibility it has been, to survive *despite the most relentless campaign of persecution* ever endured by any people, ever! The Jews have been given a *Divine mandate*. They were chosen and are still chosen and this is not, for most of them, a badge of pride or self-congratulations, it is a burden that must be reluctantly endured by most Jews, who would gladly rather sink into welcome obscurity. Witness a typical conversation between a Jew and a Gentile Christian:

Christian: God really loves the Jewish people, you know. It says so in the Scriptures.

Jew: And how does He show this love for us? Tell me, I need to know.

Christian: Well, He has made sure that, despite all that the world has thrown at you for the past 2000 years or so, you are still here. You've survived. Isn't that proof of His love?

Jew: And how does that show His love for us?

Christian: By bringing you through the troubles. Look, you've outlived the Romans, the Greeks, the Assyrians, the Babylonians, the Nazis! You've triumphed over all of them.

Jew: Triumph? I see no triumph in the ghetto, in the concentration camp. How is this triumph? We may survive these things, but only to bring us through a new set of troubles. Why can't we be like other people? To be born, to be left alone in peace and then to die of peaceful old age, just like everyone else.

Christian: But you're God's chosen people!

Jew: Chosen for what? For persecution? For hatred? As scapegoats for the world's problems? If this is what being chosen is all about, then you can keep it!

Did God choose the Jews because they were better than anyone else, or more holy, stronger, or cleverer? The Bible tells us otherwise in Chapter seven of the Book of Deuteronomy: *"The LORD did not set his affection on you and choose you because you were more numerous than other peoples, for you were the fewest of all peoples. But it was because the LORD loved you and kept the oath he swore to your ancestors that he brought you out with a mighty hand and redeemed you from the land of slavery, from the power of Pharaoh king of Egypt."*

God loved these people and there is no indication that He has stopped loving them since, despite what the rest of mankind would prefer to believe. If you are a person of faith and someone honest enough to confess a distaste for Jewish people, then this is a sobering thought. Do you really want to go against God on this issue? Food for thought.

29 Of course, I am writing these words through my own eyes of faith. You may be different. You may interpret the Bible verses differently, or you may not even see the validity of the Bible in the first case, or even accept the existence of God. If you are in this latter category then perhaps you are starting to understand – though perhaps don't agree with - the thrust of this book. The title is a giveaway, *The Jews, Your Majesty*, as an explanation for the very existence of God. Perhaps this is a good time to explore this a little more.

I repeat what I said earlier:

There has never been a satisfactory explanation for antisemitism from historians, philosophers, psychologists, sociologists, economists and social commentators, for the simple reason that it seems to be driven by *blind irrational hatred*. Can this really be orchestrated, the greatest conspiracy of all? Is this possible?

And …

We are now going to delve into the origins of this *longest hatred* and, having exhausted all natural explanations for it, confounding the historians, social scientists, psychologists, anthropologists, sociologists and anyone else with an 'ology', we are now going to enter the realm of the *supernatural*.

So, welcome to my world. You are free to leave at any time, but it would be a shame if you miss out on a few thoughts that may impact you in some way. Let's not be like those protestors mentioned earlier, happy to express themselves through slogans penned by others, rather than through personal investigation. You are better than that.

Imagine you are standing in front of a huge mountain of fine earth that is slowly emptying itself through a magic sieve into a bottomless ditch. The mountain represents the weight of evidence for the antisemitic acts committed by mankind. As the dust flows through the sieve, it recreates a visible episode of history, before it is emptied into the ditch. This is going to involve your imagination, so please bear with me here. The process starts.

The dust settles into the form of a cross, with a man, Jesus, nailed to its beam, dying horribly. His body crumbles, but the cross remains, shrinking and fashioned into a breastplate on the body of a Crusader. It is July 15th, 1099. It is the time of the First Crusade. He is in Jerusalem, on a horse, sword aloft, triumphantly wading through the blood of the Jews he and his chums have just slaughtered in a synagogue. He is joyfully singing hymns as he rides to a church to celebrate. You can imagine his thoughts; *We have avenged our Saviour, the Christ-killers have been vanquished*. As the dust siphons through the sieve, the words 'Christ Killers' are the last to disappear, as your mountain of evidence provides the first exhibit.

No sooner than this disappears we see the body of a young boy, William, from the town of Norwich. He lays still, having been hanged and buried. His figure morphs into a small mob pointing at a group of Jews. *Child killers*, is the scream. In the background a lone figure slinks away, a priest, who had actually killed the boy as a publicity stunt to put Norwich on the pilgrimage map. As the dust siphons through the sieve, the words 'Child Killers' are the last to disappear, as your mountain of evidence provides the second exhibit.

Time speeds ahead, as excuse after excuse for Jew hatred pour from the mountain to the sieve, each culminating in the accusation spelt out; *host desecrators, bringer of plagues, well poisoners, coin tamperers, friends of the devil*.

127

Eventually the mountain has levelled and perhaps we breathe a sigh of relief, that this litany of hatred has finally exhausted itself. But then we see another mountain behind it, then another one, then another one. Each represents a new set of scenarios. The first, as we saw, was the mountain representing Christian antisemitism. Then there was the mountain of the Islamists, of the Marxists, of the neo-Nazis, of the conspiracy buffs, of the United Nations, of the academics, of the left-leading media, of the student activists. Every mountain has the same fine earth, all sifted by the sieve into the ditch where it mixed with the earth already there. Although each mountain presented a different manifestation of antisemitism, the end result was the same.

Soon it had finished. Every mountain had been levelled and all we are left with is the bottomless ditch, filled with the earth. Still room left, plenty of space for more, for new expressions of this ancient hatred. Then, suddenly, there is movement. The earth erupts out of the ground into the air and, out of this a figure emerges, a figure of evil, a sum total of all of the hatred that has been poured into the earth. But who is this figure? We are soon about to find out.

Let's be clear, absolutely clear, even at the expense of drilling away endlessly at the same point. *Antisemitism makes absolutely no sense at all.* To stick your head in the sand and call it an irrelevance or just a set of co-incidences is to bypass any critical faculties you may have. It is a thing, it exists … deal with it! It has been called the many-headed hydra, cut one head off and a new one grows in its place. It has to be seen as a whole, as a single phenomenon, which means, there must be a *single mind behind it!*

30

In Derek's story earlier, Dawn had this to say at approximately the same part of the journey where we find ourselves now. This is how she explained it.

"God has this enemy ... the devil. Yes I can see that ... Who hates him ... for reasons not yet explained ... yes I can live with that. Of course, if I hated someone to that degree and saw him gathering together a group of followers, thousands of them, and declaring them 'his people forever' ... then I'm going to be more than a little miffed ... so ... it makes sense that the devil would hate the Jews and do all that he can to make their lives miserable because .... If he can't get to the Big Man ... then why not concentrate on the followers. Classic bullying behaviour, I reckon!"

The hatred against the Jews is easily explained *if you have ears to hear*. If you are willing to accept the presence of an eternal enemy, a spiritual adversary, then you must accept that the Devil's war against God is going to be played out in the world in a certain way. He is going to target God's representatives, isn't he? Just process this thought and think again if the penny hasn't yet dropped!

I have explained it in another way earlier in Derek's story and this may help you to understand it better. How have the Jews managed to survive so long despite being hated by so many people? That's the question, an obvious one really. The answer, for me, is equally obvious ... It uncovers a drama that has been unfolding for thousands of years, but which is hidden from most. The drama is a classic conflict between good and evil, between two great powers that have been in opposition since time began.

If we concede this possibility, then perhaps the evidence can start to make sense. We can see that the reason that the Jews have survived so long is that a great power has been protecting them and that the reason that they have been hated for so long is that another great power has been attacking them. This provides us with an answer to our key question.

The reason the Jews have managed to survive so long despite being hated by so many people is because the power that is protecting them is greater than the power that has been attacking them. God against Satan, the Devil. No contest.

Yes, it may seem that we have entered the realms of science fiction or even the tortured halls of the conspiracy dreamers. If you are willing to accept the possibility of God, then surely it's not a great stretch to consider the possibility of the Devil. These days he probably gets far more publicity than his adversary, looking at the growth and reach of horror books, games and movies. Where there is good, surely there must be evil too?

At the start of our journey, we considered the King's question. The existence of the Jews has been put forwards as proof of the existence of God. We can imagine him asking a second question … now this is where the rubber hits the road … 'Do you have proof for the existence of the Devil?' he asked his Christian friend. The answer now, obviously suggests itself. *Antisemitism, Your Majesty. Hatred of the Jews.*

31 Are you still with me? Just because God and the Devil may not have figured much in your life so far, it doesn't mean that they don't exist, rather that you've been looking elsewhere, or not even looking at all. But, as I said earlier, *Now Everything Changes* and perhaps there is something within you compelling you to find some answers to the madness that surrounds us these days in our culture.

Give yourself time to mull this over, but please don't dismiss this out of hand just because it is unfamiliar territory. It could well be a new road opening up for you.

There is one disclaimer, though. Those of us who believe in God have not bought into a religious system, instead we are following a single person, Jesus. Particularly on the issue of antisemitism I have to sadly declare that the majority of the church in the UK has got things so wrong. Don't blame God, or Jesus for this, just the hearts of men and women, clinging on to old prejudices, rather than basking in the freedoms of being a 'new creation.' And it's this issue that we will now investigate.

32 There is an important question that needs to be asked, why does the Church still have problems with the Jews and why does Christian antisemitism even exist? Outside of Nazi Germany, the Church has historically been *the biggest persecutor of the Jews in history,* despite claiming to follow a Jewish Messiah. I think there are five main reasons, though it wouldn't surprise me if more are found, as the Devil adapts to our changing times:

1) Jealousy
Some Christians can't believe that God would favour any people other than themselves. They believe God to be fickle enough to abandon a people whom He has clearly called *His* people.

2) Power and Greed
Christendom – State Christianity – has been no friend of the Jews, whom it has used to suit its own needs. Much of its treatment of the Jews were a deflection from its own sins, in forced conversions, expulsions, massacres and the seizure of assets.

3) Lack of understanding
Many theologians have twisted Biblical texts to boost their own negativity towards the Jews, whom they deem rejected by God.

4) Detachment from God
If a Christian has a healthy relationship with God, it will also include a positive attitude towards the Jewish people.

5) Hatred
The antisemitism virus affects everyone, including those who consider themselves born-again. No-one is immune.

We will examine each in turn. If you are a Christian, perhaps you should also examine yourself, to see if your soul has suffered contamination in any way, either through intent or ignorance. This is not a condemnation, this is simply a response to the mountain of evidence we have seen. Antisemitism is a virus, a sickness that has permeated the Church right from the beginning. It has had over 2,000 years to bed itself into the Christian psyche. The fact that the only Christians who acknowledge this, are dealing with it and are acting on it in their lives are seen as a *minority in the Body of Christ*, is a manifestation of this sickness. We must acknowledge this and deal with this, either as whistleblowers or through self-realisation.

33 There has always been jealousy of Jewish people by Christians, particularly when their own inadequacies are shown up. For instance, many early Christians looked with admiration at their Jewish neighbours and even took part in some festivals, such as Passover. The jealous Church leaders took exception to this and, at the Council of Nicaea in the 4th Century, a stop was put to this. Constantine the Great, in his letter to the Churches

'concerning the Jews' on October 18th 315 AD, stated, *"Moreover, if any one of the population should join their abominable sect and attend their meetings, he will bear with them the deserved penalties."*

Jewish life through the ages has been bittersweet. The bitterness has been from without, the sweetness from within. Their communities have always lived in a precarious state, never accepted by the Christian world that surrounded them. Yet once the outside world had been shut out, life for ordinary Jews within their own communities had been a million times more meaningful, wholesome and joyful than that of their Christian neighbours, particularly through the 'Dark Ages.' How ironic was that? So while the Christian was living in poverty, ignorance and subservience, kept in place by the promises of the "next world," what of his Jewish neighbour? Let us consider the home. When the Jerusalem Temple was destroyed by the Romans, the rabbis declared that every Jewish home should become a holy place, referring to them as a *miqdash me'at*, a "small sanctuary." The home was to be a place for worshipping God, a holy place. While the Christians at that time trapped God in cold, busy, glitzy cathedrals and churches, as the exclusive property of the clergy, with visiting rights granted to the *hoi polloi* every Sunday, in the Jewish tradition God was present in the place where they slept, ate and gathered together as families.

There were many other triggers for their jealousy, one being the small numbers of Jews succumbing to plagues such as the Black Death. It was simply because of their cleanliness laws, which their neighbours ignored and, instead, blamed the Jews for the Black Death. It has to be said that, throughout history, Jewish home life followed the Biblical norms and was far more "Christian" in behaviour and practice than their Christian counterpart. Hence the jealousy.

34 We have to face the facts, *Christendom,* State Christianity, is not the best way that our faith could have been corporately celebrated. It speaks of the establishing of a Kingdom, perhaps one *taking the appearance* of a Divine kingdom, but being run on very human lines, with very human failings. It has given us such abhorrences as the *Crusades,* an ungodly land grab, forced conversions and expulsions of the Jews and the *Inquisition,* torture in the Name of Christ! It has given us a "State Religion" (C of E) and denominations, run as political and financial corporations and currently as infiltrated by the woke agenda as all other more blatantly secular enterprises. For example, the Church of England has created a fund of one hundred million pounds as reparation for the slave trade, which it hugely profited from. This is virtual signalling through loud hailers! If this means that God's current work at the grass roots level is going to suffer because of this siphoning of funds, then one has to wonder where their wisdom comes from.

The Church has certainly profited from the slave trade over the last few hundred years, there is no denying this. But think, also, how the Church in our country also profited through their treatment of Jewish people since 1066, including the seizing of assets and expulsions. If reparations for these acts are taken into account then, as I implied earlier, the C of E (even the whole country) would probably be bankrupted overnight! But Jews never feature positively in the woke agenda that drives our culture, even the ecclesiastical outposts.

35 Now, if you have no stake in understanding the Christian position, feel free to skip forward to section 37. Of course, this may mean you missing

a gem or two, so perhaps you should speed-read the next two sections first, just in case 😊.

The majority of Christians in the UK have (possibly unknowingly in some cases) bought into something called *Replacement Theology* when considering the Jewish people. Its core feature is that the Jews have been replaced by the Church in God's plans, even *rejected* by Him in some expressions of it. This is a place of refuge for some who need to find Biblical backup for their negative views of the Jews, though we have to accept that some may be sincere in their investigations. It is not my place to refute every Biblical argument, this kind of sparring I leave to others. Instead, we need to consider any personal agenda they have in their arguments, but also – and very importantly – *the practical outcome of their beliefs*. Martin Luther, the great Christian reformer, turned against the Jews in his later years and wrote some of the most vile things about them. These were taken up hundreds of years later by Adolph Hitler, as a rubber stamp for his own practical outcomes of his Jew-hatred, reasoning that *the greatest German theologian of all time couldn't have been wrong!*

Here's a quote by one of the most influential Christian thinkers in the UK:

"What about the promised land?" Is the setting up of the State of Israel a fulfillment of prophecy? Well, I cannot go into this in a detail. I can only say this: Some people think so. ... Others, among whom I number myself, do not hold that view. I'll leave aside political questions that could occupy us for a long time, but I'll just mention to you that you need to think about political issues here. The risk of ignoring the justice of the Palestinian cause is on the one hand, and on the other is the risk of encouraging further Jewish expansionism since the land promised to Abraham in the Old Testament included territory that belongs today to

Jordan and to Lebanon and to Syria. So, beware of what you are saying if you think all that belongs to the Jews forever." John Stott, Senior Rector of All Souls Church London 1950-1975 (in a sermon "The Place of Israel" reprinted on pages 164-172 of Zion's Christian Soldiers, Stephen Sizer, IVP 2007)

John Stott was a prominent and highly respected UK Churchman. You'll notice that he is speaking about the identity of Israel rather than directly referencing the Jewish people. Yet … it is impossible theologically to separate the Jewish people from the concept and the land of Israel, as both are derived from one of the oldest prophecies in the Bible, the covenant between God and Abraham.

"As for me, this is my covenant with you: You will be the father of many nations. No longer will you be called Abram]; your name will be Abraham, for I have made you a father of many nations. I will make you very fruitful; I will make nations of you, and kings will come from you. I will establish my covenant as an everlasting covenant between me and you and your descendants after you for the generations to come, to be your God and the God of your descendants after you. The whole land of Canaan, where you now reside as a foreigner, I will give as an everlasting possession to you and your descendants after you; and I will be their God." (Genesis 17:4-8)

From Abraham, *spiritual* blessing has been given to his spiritual descendants, Christians, whether Jew or Gentile. But also, there have been *physical* blessings to his physical descendants, the Jews, whether it is the Land or fruitfulness. It is a feature of the pagan dualism that came from the Greek philosopher Plato to emphasise the "spiritual" over the "physical," which helps to explain the origins of the views expressed by those Church leaders who embrace Replacement Theology. Here is a partial list of the consequences of such thinking:

• They ignore Bible interpretation principles followed by the earliest Christians, the Protestant Reformers and Jesus himself and that is to give priority to the plain literal reading of Scripture.

• They deny God's faithfulness in not breaking His promises (covenants) with the Jews. If He could, then why couldn't He do the same with Christians?

• They don't see the Old Testament and the New Testament as a continuous whole and would rather diminish the importance of the Old Testament, a consequence of a 2nd Century heresy called Marcionism, born out of Platonism in the Early Church.

• They ignore the clear teaching in the Psalms and Prophets of God's continuous love for the Jewish people e.g. Jeremiah 31:37, *"Thus says the LORD: 'If the heavens above can be measured, and the foundations of the earth below can be explored, then I will cast off all the descendants of Israel for all that they have done, says the LORD'."*

• They fail to explain why the tradition they follow has never offered God's mercy and forgiveness to the Jewish people but has rather provided theological foundation for extreme hatred and persecution.

• They offer no reasonable explanations for the continuous existence of the Jewish people, the miraculous formation of modern Israel and the undeniable contributions of Jewish people to society.

But evidence is all very well. The real problem is at the heart of the established Church in the UK today.

So ... what *is* the story here? I pose this curious question because of a meeting that took place in 2002 between prominent Jews and Christians and which was reported by

Melanie Phillips as a feature in the Spectator entitled, *Christians who hate the Jews*.

Now that's a title that means business. It says exactly what it means and it sent a shiver through both the Jewish community, who had considered the dark days of Christian anti-Jewish feeling way gone and Church leaders, who *retreated into denial*. Yet the Christians at this meeting included Andrew White, Rowan Williams and Patrick Sookhdeo, who would have been expected to provide an acceptable consensus of the Church. Here is a short extract from the article:

The Jews at the meeting were incredulous and aghast. Surely the Christians were exaggerating. Surely the Churches' dislike of Israel was rooted instead in the settlements, the occupied territories and Prime Minister Ariel Sharon. But the Christians were adamant. The hostility to Israel within the Church is rooted in a dislike of the Jews.

Church newspaper editors say that they are intimidated by the overwhelming hostility to Israel and to the Jews from influential Christian figures, which makes balanced coverage of the Middle East impossible. Clerics and lay people alike are saying openly that Israel should never have been founded at all. One Church source said that what he was hearing was a 'throwback to the visceral anti-Judaism of the Middle Ages.'

So, some Christians hate the Jews. The problem is all theirs and one day they will have to answer to a Higher authority, particularly the teachers among them. If there has to be a single message to those who seek to replace Israel with the Church it is this; Church history has shown that the holding of certain doctrines has consequences and the holding of *this particular doctrine* has birthed horrific evil from the heart of man, culminating in the Holocaust but certainly not stopping there. Rabbi Abraham Heschel escaped from the Nazis but his mother and two of his sisters died in concentration camps. When asked if he would ever return to the places of his birth and upbringing, he replied:

"If I should go to Poland or Germany, every stone, every tree would remind me of contempt, hatred, murder, of children killed, of mothers burned alive, of human beings asphyxiated."

It's not about holding onto theological opinions and fighting your ground in the debating chambers. It is about *life and death* for some and the Church has done little to show Jesus to his own people *and is still doing little.*

36 By definition a Christian should love God and all His ways. He should also know about God's adversary, whom we have identified as the originator of antisemitism in all of its forms. This adversary, the Devil, hates God, hates His Messiah, Jesus and His people, the Church. He particularly hates the Jews. The apostle Paul, writing in the New Testament, gives us extra reasons for this:

Theirs is the adoption as sons; theirs the divine glory, the covenants, the receiving of the law, the temple worship and the promises. Theirs are the patriarchs, and from them is traced the human ancestry of Christ, who is God over all, forever praised! Amen. (Romans 9:4-5)

The Jews were responsible for all of this! No wonder the Devil hates them. He also hates them because they hold the key to his ultimate demise, when Jesus Christ returns as a Jew to the Mount of Olives in Jerusalem and claims his inheritance. And that's a whole different book!

That's the reason for antisemitism, no other is needed and it implies something too awful to contemplate:

If you have any negativity towards the Jews, even in a small way, then you are aiding and abetting the enemy of our souls.

Never before can a much-used phrase have more relevance; the uncomfortable truth. Just ask those people who are arguably closest to God of all Christians, the intercessors, those who grapple with God in prayer. You will not find a single, authentic intercessor who does not pray for the Jewish people, not as a replaced or rejected people, but as a people whom God Himself calls *the apple of my eye*. Hold on to this fact, it is a telling one.

37 Well done for reaching the end, particularly if you are one of those who was drawn in through the story of Derek and hung around to go deeper, even if this was against every instinct you thought you had. If so, then this may have been the only way you would have discovered what's really going on in the world and how antisemitism is so much at the heart of our current culture. As an illustration of this and referring back to an observation I made regarding the Eurovision Song Contest in 2024, the Swiss entry probably wouldn't have won if it weren't for world antisemitism. Hatred of Israel clearly affected the votes of the official juries, who marked Israel down as far as they could, but a reaction against antisemitism from the 'silent majority' of fair-minded people, ensured that Israel was marked up way beyond expectations. So, who knows who actually deserved to win? (not that I care one hoot!)

This book has been written for everyone, regardless of race or religion, affiliations or backgrounds. It is a story that needs to be told, at an age when truth is whatever makes you feel comfortable and whatever feeds your prejudices and desires. Absolute truth is out of favour these days but … it hasn't really ever gone away and will still be around even when the woke bubble bursts, leaving many people, at the very least, with egg on their faces!

And what is this truth anyway? One thing that we can all agree with – and I am sure that enough evidence has been produced to back this up – is that Israel and the Jews are significant. Significant enough to create the following observations:

• Israel's actions towards Hamas/Palestinians will always be centre on the world stage.

• Many people see no difference between Israelis and Jews in general, so any actions of Israel have a negative impact on Jews everywhere.

• There is a strange alliance between Islamists and the far left, despite nothing in common other than hatred of Jews.

• What is observed is just one manifestation of antisemitism, which has taken many different forms over the years.

Perhaps we can all agree on the above. It is when we dig deeper that we get into contentious areas, depending on our mindsets and what we are prepared to believe. All I have done is provide a hypothesis based on my background as a Jew who believes in Jesus. This is how I see it:

• The Jews made an agreement with God around 4,000 years ago, from which they earned their 'chosen people' tag. They agreed to be His representatives on Earth.

• This agreement is still intact, despite the presence of Christians, who are also God's representatives but do not replace the Jews. If God is fickle enough to reject the Jews 'for whatever reason' then Christians should live in fear that the same could easily happen to them, with their *chequered track record*!

- God has an adversary, the Devil, who has spent the last 4,000 years trying to rid the world of God's 'chosen people', very nearly succeeding with the Holocaust.

- God will prevail.

How you respond is totally up to you. You may just see yourself only as an interested observer, perhaps now with more understanding and even sympathy, but no intention to take this any further. This may have woken you up, as it did King Fred (or Louis) and provided you with food for thought on this 'God thing.' Perhaps you will join Derek and Dawn on the next chapter of their lives, as they follow through on the journey they have already started.

If you are a Christian and feel challenged by what you have read then perhaps, even if in a small way, you can be an agent for change within the Church. It is clear that, at the moment, the Church in our country does not 'get' the Jews and perhaps doesn't want to 'get' the Jews. Either way, this is not good and you need to realise that this state of affairs is bad news for the future of the Church.

There is still antisemitism in the Church, *there is no doubt about this.* Otherwise, we would have been seeing Israeli flags in church windows, proclamations from Church leaders that condemn terrorism (rather than condemning responses to terrorism) and marches in support of Israel and the Jews through our city centres to rival the ones for the Palestinians. We would have Church leaders demanding the return of hostages rather than as an afterthought. Antisemitism is not always intentional, but it thrives, even below the surface if it is not dealt with because that is what the Devil wants.

Am I being unnecessarily melodramatic? If I'm correct in my findings, then perhaps not dramatic enough. If your gut feeling is *why is he going on about the Jews again*, then you may have some serious self-examination to do. If you are getting irritated and peeved then, by all means get angry, but consider this; *what if he's right?* If antisemitism is truly from the Devil, then surely you want to be batting for the right side?!

The only way to be sure is to get on your knees and pray, as the intercessors do, *God, show me my heart in these matters.*

Instead, what do we see? Actions to appease Hamas and their supporters, so as not to draw too much attention to a Church that wants to be seen to be "tolerant," "relevant" and "peace-loving." But ... on October 7th, 2023 ... we had one of those pivotal points in history (the only other two I believe in living memory were 9/11 and the COVID-19 pandemic) and ... *Now everything changes!* Perhaps it will?

Do we want our leaders, whether National leaders or Church leaders, to be Neville Chamberlain telling us *"I have this piece of paper in my hand ..."* or rather Churchill *"We shall fight them on the beaches...?"* Perhaps the issue of antisemitism in our culture is just the tip of the iceberg, the symptom of an illness within our society? Perhaps Israel and the Jews are just the current front-line troops?

The fence is creaking. Too many are sitting on it. It's either one side or the other. You choose.

BOOKS

Available from good bookshops or
https://www.saltshakers.com/shop-israel-jews

Outcast Nation

The story of the People and the Land through biblical and secular history, tracing the out-workings of God's covenants and offering explanations for both the survival and the success of this Outcast Nation.

Zionion

This book scratches away at the phenomenon known as antisemitism and takes an intelligent and balanced approach to arrive at the real heart of the matter.

BOOKLETS

Available from good bookshops or
https://www.saltshakers.com/shop-israel-jews

The Simple guide to the Middle East Conflict

Much heat has been generated by the subject of Israel and Palestine. This 8-page booklet has provides a simple but effective introduction to this complex issue.

For whatever reason

This booklet outlines the spiritual root of the current Israel/Palestine crisis - it is taken from a chapter of the book, The Bishop's New Clothes.

YOUTUBE VIDEO

Blindspot

Available at blindspot.church

This short, hard-hitting and entertaining video will surprise and shock you if you think all is well in the Western Church. It arrives at the heart of the problem between the Church and Israel through a surprising route. It should have particular use in trying to reach younger Christians, from Generation X, Y and Z, who tend to be the hardest to reach on this particular subject!

WEB APP

The Mirror

Available at themirror.church

The World, with all of its burdens and intrigues, spins on its axis. Where is this axis located? Apparently, a tiny strip of land between Israel and Egypt. The goings-on in Gaza tugs at the emotions like none other. Despite over a million Muslim refugees about to be expelled by Pakistan, the repression of millions of Muslim Uyghurs in China, the bombing of Ukraine by Russia and over a hundred other armed conflicts around the world only one issue will regularly bring out tens of thousands of indignant protesters to the streets of London and other places. But it doesn't end there, as many have felt empowered to take it further, with worrying consequences. Emotions are rife, but how many really know the context of what they are protesting against?

Would you like to understand more? If so …